Texas
Fever

Texas
Fever

by

Donald Hamilton

WALKER AND COMPANY
NEW YORK

First published in the United States of America
in 1960 by Fawcett Gold Medal Books.

Published simultaneously in Canada by John Wiley & Sons, Canada,
Limited, Rexdale, Ontario.

ISBN: 0-8027-4002-2

Library of Congress Catalog Card Number: 81-69104

Printed in the United States of America

10   9   8   7   6   5   4   3   2   1

1.

Tʜɪs ᴡᴀs ᴛʜᴇ ꜱᴜᴍᴍᴇʀ of the year 1867, the third summer of peace—the third summer in which Texas men, civilians again in a land impoverished by war, had been free to drive their half-wild cattle up the long trail, known as the Shawnee Trail, that led from far below the Brazos all the way to Baxter Springs in Kansas and on up to the railroad at Sedalia, Missouri. They had been free, that is, to try. . . .

Chuck McAuliffe watched his father come riding in towards the wagon, past the edge of the herd now bedding down for the night with two riders on guard, one of them Chuck's brother Dave. In the fading light, the Old Man's straight-backed, cavalry-officer style of riding made him look even taller than his six feet three. The empty, pinned-up sleeve of his gray army coat fluttered in the evening breeze as he checked his mount and stepped from the saddle, performing each action with the careful calculation of a man who still had to remind himself that he had only one hand to work with. Chuck went forward to take the horse.

"Turn him out with the remuda and throw my saddle on the black," Jesse McAuliffe said curtly.

"Yes, sir," Chuck said, and began at once to strip the saddle from the sweaty pony.

The Old Man started off, but checked himself and turned back. "No," he said, "not like that. I appreciate your indefatigable industry, boy, but just this once take it kind of easy, like you had all night. And maybe you'd better not saddle up again until it's too dark for anybody out there to see what you're doing." He threw a casual glance back the way he'd come. "Tell the boys, when they get their night horses, to make it look lazy and peaceful. And tell them, when they turn in, to leave their trousers on, or they're apt to find themselves riding in their drawers. Got that?"

5

"Yes, sir," Chuck said.

Before the war, he'd have asked questions. Before the war, his father had been a genial and kindly man, and he'd been an eleven-year-old sprout with a large and uncontrollable curiosity. He still had the curiosity at eighteen, but it was halter-broke now; and the Jesse McAuliffe who'd come back from the war had been a grim and sarcastic and domineering person who displayed a sharp impatience towards unnecessary questions, and a kind of cool aloofness towards the son who'd stayed home.

Well, if that was the way he wanted it, Chuck thought, that was the way he could damn well have it. He, Chuck McAuliffe, had got along pretty well for four years without any paternal pats on the back, and he could continue to do so as long as necessary.

The Old Man hesitated, as if about to speak again, but turned and strode away. Watching him go, Chuck wondered just what he'd found, scouting ahead, to justify this preparedness. Indian sign, probably, and in the morning there'd be the usual collection of greasy, arrogant, armed bucks coming to exact their toll from this herd passing through their country. That is, if they couldn't manage to stampede it tonight and make off with a big bunch of strays in the confusion.

Chuck restrained himself from glancing uneasily at the patches of woods that dotted these grassy bottomlands, any one of which, here in Indian Territory, could conceal a party of beef-hungry savages. He did, however, permit himself a possessive look towards the herd. A man couldn't help a feeling of pride, he reflected, looking at that bunch of misbegotten longhorns, still not much more tame than when they'd been hazed out of the south Texas mesquite—or necked to oxen and dragged out, those that were too mean to move under their own power. They hadn't wanted to come, and all along the way it seemed as though neither man nor nature had wanted to let them through. But here they were, on the north bank of the Arkansas. The last great river barring the trail north was behind them.

It had been a drive to write home about, Chuck thought, had anybody stayed at home to receive a letter. They'd had enough rain to drown a herd of bayou alligators, and enough thunder and lightning to celebrate the Fourth of July for a century to come. They'd had Indians and stampedes in full measure, and rivers running bank-full to boot. They were short a hundred and eighty head of cattle and one man, who'd drowned at the crossing of the Red. But there were still some twelve hundred big steers left, worth at least twenty dollars apiece at the railroad, and Kansas was practically in sight—well, less than a week away, given reasonable progress.

As he unsaddled his father's horse, Chuck remained aware of the Old Man walking stiffly towards the fire. Joe Paris—back home he was ranch foreman—got up to meet him. The two men held a consultation, Jesse McAuliffe gave some instructions, and Joe went off to carry them out.

The Old Man walked over to speak to Miguel Apodaca, a small, dark rider who'd been hired on for the drive mainly because he'd claimed to have been over this trail recently—not that he wasn't a good top hand as well. But there was some mystery about Miguel and the scar that twisted one side of his face and he wasn't really popular with the crew, most of whom had worked together before the war. For one thing, Miguel had never volunteered any information about the outfit he'd accompanied to Missouri the previous year, nor would he speak of his experiences along the trail. Even in a land where a man's private business was his own, his taciturnity seemed a little overdone.

That he'd been this way before was clear, however; several times his accurate knowledge of the country had saved them time and trouble. Now he nodded, acknowledging the orders that had been given him. The Old Man stood in thought for a moment, rubbing the stump of his left arm, which gave him constant pain; then he moved wearily towards the wagon, where the cook had his supper waiting.

One hand, Chuck thought soberly, his youthful resentment fading—one hand, this herd of cattle, a handful of loyal men, and two sons. That was about all Jesse McAuliffe had left. There had been more before the war, of course, much more. There had been three sons then, but Jim, the oldest, had been killed at Gaines' Mill quite early in the war. There had been Chuck's mother, but, never strong, she'd died of grief and deprivation a year later.

There had been a fine ranch once, but after years of neglect the big house on Clear Creek stood shabby and forlorn; and land and cattle down in Texas didn't count for much these days. You could eat only so much beef, and what else could you do with a critter if you couldn't sell it? And who in Texas had money to buy? The only money left in the land was Yankee money, and to get it you had to go clear to Missouri. Well, Chuck reflected with satisfaction, it was beginning to look almost as if they might make it at that. A few half-tame Indians couldn't stop them now, Cherokees, Choctaws, Creeks, or whatever. It wasn't as if they had the real warrior tribes to worry about, like the Kiowas and Comanches farther west. . . .

Later, with darkness solid about him, he was carrying wood to the fire when Joe Paris stopped him. "Let it die down," Joe said. "Get in your blankets and act like you're asleep."

Chuck said, "That won't be hard." He set down the load of wood, and straightened up to look at Joe, whom he'd known all his life—a spare, dry man with pale, thinning hair and pale blue eyes. He could reveal to Joe the curiosity he'd never betray to the Old Man, and he said, "If it's Indians, Dad's taking them mighty serious all of a sudden. Must have come across the tracks of a big bunch out there."

"Indians?" Joe said. "Who said anything about Indians? If anything happens, stick close to the Major and forget about the herd. Them's orders."

"What about the horses?"

"Let 'em go, too, for the time being. Now get in your blankets, but keep your pistol handy and your eyes open. You can catch up on your sleep next winter."

Chuck grimaced as the older man moved away. These old-timers were always saying how you could catch up on your sleep next winter. Maybe it had seemed funny to somebody, once. He yawned and moved towards his bedroll, and yawned again, picking his way among the blanketed forms sprawled around the dying fire. They'd all been alerted. From a distance, no doubt, they looked like tired men resting after a hard day's work, dead to the world; but when you were among them you could sense that they were awake and waiting.

"Watch where you put your feet, kid!"

"If you didn't cover so damn much ground," Chuck
shot back, "you wouldn't get stepped on, Turkey."

He started to spread his blankets, yawning again—
not from sleepiness, he realized now, but because he was
tense and expectant and a little scared, not knowing
exactly what they were all waiting for. When somebody
grabbed his shoulder, he reached for the big cap-and-
ball Remington at his hip as he turned.

"What—"

The bulky shape of the cook towered over him.
"Where's that wood I told you to fetch, kid? You planning on letting that fire go plumb out?"

He was getting a little fed up with this fat cook and
his domineering ways, but he kept his voice low. "Joe
said let it burn down."

"The hell he did! How does he expect a man to keep
coffee hot—"

Joe Paris' voice reached them softly. "Shut up, Coosie.
Go play with your pots and pans."

"Ah—"

The cook released Chuck and moved away towards
the wagon, growling like a bear. Chuck watched him
grimly. He didn't mind working with the horses so much,
he told himself, although the job of wrangler was generally given to a half-grown kid or some broken-down
cowhand who could no longer do a day's work with the
herd. Well, he was the youngest in the outfit, and it was
fair enough, he supposed, although it went hard to be
treated like a kid again after he'd run the ranch for four
years while the older men were away at war.

Fair? he thought wryly. They'd got the riding and the
shooting and the glory. They'd got to fight Yankees while
he was working his head off trying to keep the place up
after a fashion. Then, after getting thoroughly licked,
they'd come straggling home, expecting him to look after
their saddle stock and fetch wood and water while they
stood around criticizing the way things had been let go
to hell. Sometimes he even got the idea the Old Man
blamed him for his mother's death.

Chuck shook his head irritably in the darkness. The
Old Man wasn't really to blame, he supposed. You had
to make allowances. You couldn't blame him for being
kind of sour, after losing almost everything. And somebody had to ride herd on the horses and do the chores

around camp. But if that lard-assed cook didn't keep his fat hand where it belonged, he was going to get it shot off. . . .

He must have made some kind of an angry sound, because there was a rustle of movement beside him and a chuckle.

"What's the matter?" It was the voice of his brother. "Coosie been riding you again?"

"Some," Chuck said.

Dave laughed, squatting down beside him. "Don't let him rile you. If the man wasn't a misfit, he wouldn't be cook for a mangy outfit like this, would he?"

Dave rolled a cigarette and took a smoldering branch from the fire to light it. The stick, breathed upon, burst into flame, showing his face briefly, bold and dark. He was tall, like their father, with a reckless and dashing air, even in his worn range clothes. Chuck couldn't help a moment of envy, wishing he'd been born to resemble his older brother, instead of being, as he was, the sickly runt of the litter. Maybe that was another reason the Old Man never had much to do with him these days: he'd never grown to look much like a real McAuliffe.

Dave blew a smoke ring that drifted across the glowing coals and was dispersed by the updraft of hot air. "Seems nice and quiet out there, doesn't it?" he said idly.

Chuck asked, "What's up? I was figuring, the way Dad was acting, it was those sneaky savages again, but Joe said—"

"Indians don't ride shod horses," Dave said. "There's worse things than redskins along this border. Well, the Old Man's usually got a trick or two up his sleeve." He yawned audibly, dismissing the subject, and asked in a different tone: "What are you planning to do when we hit Sedalia? I don't figure we'll waste any time in Baxter—anyway, they tell me that's not much of a town for pleasure—but we'll make up for it when we've got rid of the herd and have those Yankee dollars in our pockets, eh? What's the first thing you're going to do?"

Chuck scratched himself under the armpit. "Why, I kind of figured I'd take a bath," he said. "And then maybe I'll get me something to eat that wasn't fried in axle-grease."

"Sounds good as far as it goes," Dave said. "I was

kind of figuring on a little something to drink, too. About time you learned how, don't you think? Any other plans?"

"Well, no," Chuck admitted. "I hadn't thought any farther than that."

Dave laughed. "I reckon we can find you something to occupy your leisure hours, if we put our minds to it. They tell me Sedalia's quite a town. It's about time you got some education, Charley boy."

"Ma taught me to read real good," Chuck said rather stiffly. "And I can figure better than you."

Dave laughed and clapped him on the back. "I had a different kind of education in mind, Sonny," he said. He rose and tossed his cigarette into the fire. "Well, Sam and Lacey are with the herd. I reckon I'll take a little look around. Don't let Coosie worry you. If you'd been eating his cooking as long as he has, you'd hate everybody, too."

He chuckled, and vanished into the darkness. Chuck heard him reach his horse and ride off. He hadn't been gone five minutes—Chuck had barely had time to get comfortable in his blankets—when the night erupted with the thunder of hoofs and the crash of gunfire.

2.

THEY CAME in from the north, in a bunch, whooping and firing. There seemed to be dozens of them, and Chuck threw off his blankets and drew his pistol as he rose. He looked around for guidance, uncertain whether he was supposed to run for his horse or seek cover and prepare to help stand off the attack. But the yelling mass of horsemen out in the dark veered sharply before coming within range of the camp. Chuck caught a glimpse of Joe Paris, gun in hand, racing towards the picket line, and followed.

The herd had come to its feet at the first outburst of firing. It stood only a moment longer before it broke.

Chuck heard the night-guard's familiar shout: "Roll out and ride, you loafers, they're running!"

He was already at his horse. As he swung into the saddle, the animal, well-trained, pivoted to go with the cattle as it had done on other nights like this—to flank them, head them, turn them, mill them—and he had to pull it down hard while he looked for the Old Man. The ground vibrated with the rumble of the stampede as the fear-crazed steers hit their stride; their long horns clashed and clattered. They were headed upriver. By the sound of them they were set to run all night, but orders were to leave them, and Chuck fought his pony around and headed for the tall figure on the black horse.

Other McAuliffe riders were converging on the Old Man now, and he led them, first, in a direction parallel to the track of the stampede. Then, surprisingly, he turned away from the noise and confusion, swinging gradually away from the river. He brought them to a halt, finally, in a shallow depression between two low hills, black against the night sky. There were some blasphemous protests as the horsemen in the rear, not catching the signal in time, over-rode those in front. Jesse McAuliffe surveyed them from his saddle.

"You're a fair bunch of cowhands," he said dryly, "but you'd make damn poor cavalry. Now check your weapons while we rest our horses and give our friends out yonder a little time to be clever."

Chuck pulled out his cap-and-ball Remington again. It was a present from Dave, who'd taken a matched pair from a Union officer. He checked the percussion caps, spun the cylinder, and thrust the piece back into the holster with a hand that was, for some reason, a little damp and sweaty, although the night was not warm. All around him he could hear the creak of leather and the click of steel as others made similar inspections. Over it all was a rumbling sound, like distant thunder; that was the herd, still going strong to the west. There was an occasional shot out there, no telling whose.

Somebody said irritably, "Those cattle are going to be scattered to hell and gone, come morning."

The Old Man said, "Dave's got two good hands to help him. They'll do what they can."

Joe Paris, who'd ridden up the slope a ways, whistled softly to attract their attention. "Miguel's coming, Major."

"About time," the Old Man said.

They sat in silence, waiting for the little, scarred Mexican rider to reach them. He rode up, removed his wide hat, and wiped the perspiration from his forehead before speaking. The Old Man made no move to hurry him.

Miguel put his hat back on. "It is the same trick as before, *señor*," he said. "They start the herd running, but they do not follow. Instead, they ride back to camp, to await our return. There are some, armed with rifles, concealed in the wagon—the cook I did not see, he must have found a place to hide—and the rest of those *hombres* are waiting in the trees along the river within easy gunshot. If anybody rides into that camp unawares, *Señor* McAuliffe, he will be shot to ribbons."

The Old Man rubbed the stump of his arm. "In the wagon, you say, Mike?"

"*Si, señor.* Four or five of them."

"And their horses?"

"All the horses are being held by two men, just around the bend of the river to the east."

"Good enough," the Old Man said. He straightened up to regard the crew. "It's an ambush, as you've heard," he said. "They stampeded the herd to decoy us away from camp, so they could be ready and waiting when we straggled back by twos and threes."

Somebody asked, "Who are these fellows anyway, Major? You say they're white men?"

The Old Man nodded towards Miguel Apodaca. "Tell them, Mike."

Miguel said deliberately, "There are many bad men along these borders since the war—since before the war. Once, perhaps, they claimed to be fighting for one cause or another, but now they are all outlaws together. Many of them have joined, I think, to prey on the Texas trail herds. Bushwhackers, border ruffians, they are called. Last year I came this way with a dozen *compadres* and twenty-seven hundred head of cattle, property of *Señor* Peter Laughlin—"

"Old Pete Laughlin!" somebody said. "He never returned to Texas, or any of the men with him!"

"One did," Miguel said. "I did. We crossed the Arkansas about this time of year, maybe a little later. When the herd was stampeded, like tonight, we rode with it. The first men to return to camp were taken prisoner, bound and gagged. The rest, riding in unsuspecting, were shot down in cold blood. Then the prisoners were shot, too. The bodies were thrown into the river." The little rider touched his scarred face. "I was not dead, not quite. I managed to swim ashore. I made my way to Fort Gibson, downstream. Later, I returned to Texas. Those men were my friends. There is a debt to pay. *Señor* McAuliffe was the first who would listen to me, and promise me an opportunity to strike back."

There was a little silence, then the Old Man said, "Seems like some folks, when they get a trick that works, don't know when to quit using it. I figure we can at least persuade these gentlemen to change their tactics for the next herd that comes along." He cleared his throat, and spoke more briskly. "I think we should first take a little ride through camp, single file, keeping the wagon between us and the woods as much as possible. Concentrate your fire on the Yankee scum in the wagon. You won't be able to hit anything off in the trees, from horseback, anyway. They're not apt to hit you either, if you keep moving. But perforate that wagon thoroughly, hear? We'll make just one run past it, Indian fashion, but you'd better shoot better than most redskins or those bushwhackers are going to cut you to pieces. Once past, we'll swing wide, reload, and head around the bend to drive off the horses. That'll put our friends on foot. Maybe we can do some more damage while they're hunting themselves something to ride." The Old Man paused. "Any questions?"

There were no questions. Jesse McAuliffe gave a signal, and they were riding again. Chuck found that his mouth was very dry; when somebody pulled alongside, he was more startled than there was any sense in being, and angry with himself to boot.

Joe Paris asked, "Scared, boy?"

He shook his head quickly. "No."

The older man grinned in the darkness. "That makes you either a liar or a fool. Well, you've been complaining because the war got over before you got to shoot at a Yankee. Now you'll have a chance to see what you missed. Just keep your interval and keep riding. Remember that not many men can hit a fast-moving target in the dark, at any distance, particularly if it's shooting back. Don't open fire until you know you're in range. If your horse goes down, take cover behind it and make yourself as small as possible. Most likely somebody'll

come back for you. We can't afford to break in another
wrangler."

Paris gave him a whack on the shoulder and rode ahead
to join the Old Man again. Chuck wondered briefly if his
father had sent the foreman back to encourage him. It
didn't seem likely; the Old Man hadn't even turned his
head. Then something else drove the question from
his mind. The camp was in sight ahead: the low fire and
the innocent-looking, deserted wagon. Beyond was the
black mass of trees, silent, waiting.

They were in single file now, riding well strung out.
The Old Man led them in at an easy trot, at an angle.
There was no sound or movement in the camp. They
would be waiting to spring their trap, Chuck thought;
they couldn't tell, from the sound, in the darkness, how
many men were riding into their guns.

The first shot was the Old Man's, at long pistol range,
and the whole column surged ahead. Then Joe Paris
was in range and firing, and still there was no answer
from the wagon or the trees, and Chuck had time to
think how silly they'd all feel if there should be nobody
there, and they'd have shot hell out of an empty wagon
—their own wagon at that. Even as the thought crossed
his mind, the dirty canvas went up and a ragged sheet
of flame blazed from the side of the standing vehicle.

Yellow spurts of flame blossomed in the woods beyond.
It seemed impossible that the leaders of the column
could escape that concentrated fire, but they were still
riding, still shooting, and now the man ahead of Chuck
was in range, and Chuck had his own gun ready as he
swept in at full gallop. The big Remington pistol was
bucking in his hand. . . .

He didn't realize, until he was out again, that he'd
been yelling—they'd all been screaming like banshees—
and the high rebel yell still hung in the air as the Mc-
Auliffe rider at the tail of the column threw his fire into
the riddled wagon that no longer answered back. Well
away from the trees, the Old Man brought them to a
halt.

"Reload!" he snapped, rising in the stirrups to look
them over. "Anybody hit too bad to ride?"

There was no answer, only the bellows-like breathing
of the horses, the steady rustle of movement, and occasional metallic sounds, as fresh loads were rammed
home into fouled chambers. Chuck juggled powder-flask

and bullet-pouch desperately in the dark. He had time to recharge only three chambers of his weapon before they were riding again.

He could never recall the exact details of the rest of the night, except that his gun was never again fully loaded. It seemed as if he was leaving a trail of spilled powder and percussion caps clear across Indian Territory. When they scattered the horses he was only vaguely aware of it; he knew there must have been a lot of subsequent riding and shooting; mostly he remembered the night as a frantic struggle to keep up with the rest of the crew while trying to cram fresh charges into an eternally empty weapon.

The Old Man pulled them off at last, saying that the bushwhackers still outnumbered them two to one, and if they kept in pursuit they might well run into a trap. They rode back towards camp, reaching it just at daybreak. A dejected, muddy figure was sitting by the fire: the cook, who'd taken shelter in the river, shaking with cold. There was some laughter at this, but it died when they saw the wagon. Of the five men it had contained, not one had escaped. They lay in the splintered wagon-bed as death had found them. The ground beneath was red.

There was a little silence, then somebody sighed, and little Miguel Apodaca brushed the scar on his face thoughtfully with his fingertips, and said in a tentative voice: "The river is very near."

The Old Man said, "We'll give them a Christian burial, little though they deserve it."

"*Si, señor*. I will take on shovel. This is a grave I will dig with pleasure."

The Old Man said, "Pat, Turkey, give him a hand."

Turkey LeBow, a middle-aged rider with a long neck and a prominent Adam's apple, said without emphasis, "Be glad to oblige, but I've got an arm that quit working a while back. Seems to be a hole in it." He swayed in the saddle as he spoke.

"Help him down," the Old Man said. "Get him over by the fire and fetch my tools and I'll have a look. . . . Anybody else? Well, as we used to say during the war, if you can't be bullet-proof, it helps to be lucky. Coosie, you stop shaking and rustle up some hot water and coffee. Chuck, you get after that remuda, boy. We're still in the cattle business, in case you'd forgotten, and we're going to need fresh horses as soon as we hear from . . ."

Joe Paris, who'd ridden to a nearby point of vantage, whistled softly. "Rider coming in, Major."

The Old Man's voice was even. "Dave?"

"No, sir. Looks like Sam Biederman." Joe hesitated, and cleared his throat. "But he's leading a pony with something across the saddle, wrapped in a slicker. . . ."

3.

Jesse McAuliffe turned his horse without a word, heading out to meet the incoming rider. After a moment, Chuck kicked his own tired mount into motion and followed. The rest of the crew remained where they were, not wishing to intrude on a family matter. The Old Man did not glance aside when Chuck caught up with him. On the rise west of camp, they reined in, having come far enough to recognize the lead animal as Dave's bay night horse. They waited without speaking until Sam Biederman reached them.

Sam was a big blond man with a red and normally cheerful face, but his features were grim and hard now. He met the Old Man's look, shook his head, and looked away. Jesse McAuliffe dismounted deliberately and walked forward to move the folds of the slicker aside. He stood there for several seconds in silence, then replaced the slicker the way it had been. When he spoke, his voice was quiet.

"Where did you find him?"

"Only about a mile out, it was," Sam Biederman said. "Lacey, he is with the main bunch of cattle, upstream. Dave we never saw after the first mix-up. When light come, I ride back to look. The pony was just standing there."

"Powder burns," the Old Man said.

Sam nodded. "I think he must have run right into one of them in the dark, maybe after they turned back. Empty his gun was, and in his hand."

The Old Man nodded. He said quietly, "We'll bury him up here on higher ground. Chuck, fetch my Bible . . . and, Chuck. . . ."

"Yes, sir."

"Tell Miguel we'll be needing the shovels here." The Old Man's voice was steady enough, but a hint of strong emotion ran through it. "He can use the river for his chore, like he wanted to. I don't want those Yankees lying in the same ground."

It didn't take long. When the time came, the Old Man read a few words from the Bible. His voice was quite flat and emotionless now.

They spent the next two days rounding up strays. It was raining the morning they hit the trail again, leaving the crude wooden cross behind them. They could see it for a couple of hours through the rain; then a low ridge blocked it from view.

"Chuck," Joe Paris said, riding alongside, "never look back."

"No, sir," Chuck said.

"Get up there with the drag. Turkey's taking over supervision of these broomtails until his arm heals."

"Yes, sir," Chuck said.

Joe Paris grimaced. "Don't try that phony humility on me, bub. It's been yessir and nosir ever since we left Texas. What are you trying to prove, anyway?"

"Prove?" Chuck said. "I'm not trying to prove anything."

Joe glanced ahead to where Jesse McAuliffe was riding. "So he didn't appreciate all the hard work you'd put into the place while he was away, is that it? He maybe made some comment that the house needed painting, or that there seemed to be a hell of a lot of unbranded stock running around. And maybe he wasn't as patient with damn-fool questions about the war as he should have been. Don't any of us like to talk about it much." Chuck didn't speak, and Joe went on: "Did it maybe occur to you that he hadn't had it so easy himself for those four years? I can tell you; I was with him. And a man who comes back from a war is seldom the same man who went away, particularly when he's had the job of leading other men to their death. And what he comes back to generally isn't what it was, either."

Chuck said dryly, "He made that clear enough, for a fact."

"I wasn't referring to the ranch," Joe said. "I was referring to you, bub. He left an eleven-year-old kid behind

and returned to find a fifteen-year-old sprout with a
chip on his shoulder and the notion he ought to be treated with consideration and respect, like a grown man. So
you got off on the wrong foot, right at the start, both of
you. He'd been giving orders for four years and so, by
God, had you, in your little way, around the ranch. You'd
been the man of the place, and you weren't in a hurry to
play second or third fiddle gracefully. Dave declared
himself out, being an easygoing sort, but you and the
Major . . . you weren't either of you going to give an
inch, you damn stubborn McAuliffes. So you've been
feuding politely for close onto three years now."

"Wouldn't call it a feud, exactly," Chuck protested.

"Call it what you please," Joe snapped. "You know
what I mean. And then this drive came along, and you
got stuck with the job of wrangler, which hurt your dignity some more, and it's been yessir and nosir ever since.
How long are you planning to keep it up, boy? You're
about all the family he's got left, now, and he's about all
the family you've got left. One of you is going to have
to make the first move, and you're a lot younger than he
is. Think it over, and now get the hell on up there and
see if the rumps of those cattle look so much better
than the rear ends of these horses. . . ."

That night, fifteen miles north of the river, the rain
turned into a regular deluge accompanied by a display of
thunder and lightning to beat anything they'd met so far.
The longhorns put up with it for a while; then a bolt of
lightning struck nearby and they were gone. They ran all
that night. Every time they were stopped, another lightning flash would stampede them again. By morning the
herd was scattered all over the countryside.

It took another two days to get it back together again
and on the trail. The weather had cleared now, and
Chuck rode along, numb with weariness, but grateful
for the warmth of the sun on his head and shoulders.
Maybe, he thought hopefully, with a couple of days like
this, they'd get to sleep in dry blankets for a change, assuming that an opportunity to sleep ever presented itself.
He wasn't aware, particularly, when the Old Man returned from one of his frequent scouting expeditions,
but presently Joe Paris came riding back to the drag.

"The Major says there's a wagon in trouble over that
way," he reported, pointing to the northeast. "Got a

woman with it, he says. She's probably some Yankee
settler's wife, old as Christmas and ugly as sin, but any
woman ought to be a welcome change from the view
you've got here." He looked at the lean steers shuffling
on ahead, tails swinging. "Come on, let's go take a
look."

They rode off across the rolling land. Chuck found
himself yawning wide enough to dislocate his jaw. If an
angel from Heaven were to appear before him—which
wasn't likely, here in Indian Territory—he didn't think
he'd be greatly interested. All he really wanted was sleep.

They found the wagon readily enough, in a hollow,
where anybody should have had sense enough not to
drive a vehicle after a spell of wet weather. It was a light
farm wagon with a canvas-covered bed, and the tires
were much too narrow for rough going—a regular butcher-
knife wagon. It was bogged down quite thoroughly. The
horses had quit and were just standing there patiently in
the mud in spite of the angry figure in skirts tugging and
beating at them—probably swearing at them, too, although the sound didn't carry. There didn't seem to be
anybody else around.

"A woman all alone out here?" Joe Paris said skeptically. "Doesn't seem likely. Could be somebody staked
out in those trees. Keep your eyes open . . . Wait a
minute. Here." He held out a handful of paper cartridges. "Noticed you were having some trouble with
that .44 of yours the other night. These'll fit; they were
Dave's. Just be sure to puncture the paper and spill
some loose powder down the chamber before you ram
the load home, or you're apt to get a misfire. Wouldn't
hurt to try a couple of shots when you get a chance. These
long conical bullets most likely won't shoot the same
as the round balls you've been using."

"Thanks," Chuck said.

"Let's ride in easy," Joe said. "That female doesn't
seem in the best frame of mind, and there's a shotgun
on the wagon seat."

They went down the slope at an easy trot. The woman
did not see them until they were almost upon her. Then
she looked around, turned, and tried to get the shotgun, but the mud and her long skirts combined to hold
her back, and Chuck rode in fast and managed to
snatch the weapon away just as she was reaching for it.

His horse brushed against her, and she was forced to cling to the muddy wagon wheel to keep from falling.

"I'm real sorry, ma'am," he said quickly. "I didn't mean—"

His voice trailed off. She wasn't at all the kind of woman he'd expected to find out here—it was an odd place to meet any woman, at all. She was smaller than he'd thought, and her hair, loose and disheveled about her shoulders, was a kind of chestnut color that threw reddish glints in the sunshine.

She wasn't dressed like any settler woman he'd ever seen. Her dark green dress was disordered and muddy now, to be sure, but he could see that it had originated as a fashionable and expensive traveling costume of fine material. She shivered as she clung there, her face hidden from him. Then she drew herself up with an effort, and swung around to face him.

"I declare, I should have known some of you beasts would sneak back to find us!" she cried. "Well, you have the gun; I reckon I can't fight you. Do what you want, just leave Papa alone this time, hear? You've hurt him enough!"

4.

THERE WAS a brief silence, while they absorbed the implications of her soft, slurred manner of speech as well as the meaning of her actual words. Then Joe Paris laughed quickly.

"Well, I do declare!" he said with his broadest drawl. "I do declare, if it isn't a little old southern girl! Where are you from, ma'am?"

She stared up at them and licked her dry lips. "You aren't—" she whispered. "You won't—"

Chuck said, in what he hoped was a reassuring tone, "I don't know who you were expecting, ma'am, but there's no need to be afraid. We're from the McAuliffe outfit: nine . . . eight men, twelve hundred longhorns, bound for Sedalia. They'll be coming along soon. You'd be seeing the dust now, if the ground wasn't wet."

"Texans?" she whispered. "Oh, thank God!"

Abruptly, she went to her knees, buried her face in her muddy hands, and began to cry. Chuck threw a quick glance towards Joe Paris, who shrugged his shoulders helplessly. Chuck looked down uncertainly at the weeping girl. It seemed indecent to leave her kneeling there, and he thrust the shotgun at Joe, dismounted, picked her up, and carried her up the slope to dry ground.

She might be smaller than he'd thought at first, but he quickly discovered that she was by no means ethereal: there was a firm little body inside the disheveled fine clothes. His breathing was somewhat labored by the time he laid her down in the shade of a nearby tree—not entirely, he realized with shame, because of his exertions. The ranch had been a man's world since his mother died. There had been few women in the neighborhood, and it had been a long time since he'd even spoken to one, let alone held one in his arms. When he straightened up, his face was hot with embarrassment, and he knew that his ears were red.

Joe Paris' voice was a welcome distraction. "There's a man in the wagon," Joe called. "Middle-aged fellow, all bandaged up. Seems to be pretty sick."

The girl had stopped crying, and was looking up at Chuck in a half-afraid, half-wondering way. Her eyes were kind of a hazel color. She might be pretty, he decided, once she washed her face—even streaked with dirt and tears, it wasn't entirely unattractive. Her lips moved.

"Papa," she whispered. "The bullet's still in his leg. I didn't know how . . . I didn't dare try . . . And he was hit on the head, too. Those brutes! He was unconscious for hours. I . . . I thought he was dying. I was trying to reach Fort Gibson with him, but it rained and the country all looked alike. . . . I don't suppose you have a doctor. . . ." Her voice died away.

Chuck said, "No, ma'am, but the Old Man's pretty handy with all kinds of wounds—that's my dad. He'll be here shortly, I reckon. He's the one that spotted you and sent us over to help."

"Oh," she said. "I saw a man on horseback, that's why I drove down here, to hide in the trees. I thought he was one of them, the men who attacked us. I didn't realize the ground would be so soft down here, and the team was almost played out, anyway. . . ." She was trying to sit up. Chuck helped her awkwardly. She pushed the thick, tangled masses of her hair back from her face, and gasped when she saw the condition of her costume. "Heavens!" she exclaimed in a stronger voice. "I looked wretched enough this morning, after being rained on for days, but now you'd think I'd been wallowing with the pigs!"

"I'll fetch some water," Chuck said quickly. "You stay right here and rest, ma'am. We'll have your wagon out in two shakes."

It took a little longer than that; but the Old Man came riding over with a couple of hands to see what was keeping them so long, and with one man to handle the team, and a pair of tough Texas ponies—accustomed to dealing with mired-down cattle—throwing their weight on ropes, they broke the rig loose and hauled it out on solid ground. The girl came running from where she'd been standing with the Old Man and climbed inside.

"Anything we can do, ma'am?" Chuck asked presently, looking into the rear of the wagon.

The man inside, hearing his voice, tried to sit up. Chuck saw a long, pale, whiskered face topped by a bandage that seemed to have been torn from some feminine garment. It gave an odd rakish look to the sunken features below.

"John Netherton," the man whispered. "My daughter Amanda . . . extremely grateful . . ."

"Lie down, Papa," the girl said. "Everything is going to be fine."

The sick man lay back and closed his eyes. The girl pulled up the blanket to cover him, and made her way back to the rear of the wagon. Chuck helped her to the ground. The Old Man came forward.

"You say you were bound for Fort Gibson when some men attacked you, Miss Netherton?"

"Why, yes," she said. "It was the second or third day after we left Baxter Springs, I've kind of lost count —the second, I think. These men came riding up, there must have been twenty of them, at least. They looked as if they'd been in some kind of a fight and got the worst of it; some were wounded and some were riding double. They were going to take our horses. . . ."

"Sounds like you encountered the same bunch that tried to ambush us by the river," Chuck said.

She glanced at him. "Well, whatever you did to them

didn't put them in any pleasant mood, I can tell you! Papa
had me hide in the wagon, but they found me and . . .
and it kind of took their mind off horses, for a spell." She
flushed. "They started by making me cook and serve for
them. . . . they threw everything out of the wagon, our
provisions, my trunk, Papa's instruments and books—
he's an engineer and surveyor by profession. They broke
open my trunk and . . . and made sport with all my
pretty things. You know what a bunch of drunken ruffians would think was funny, parading around with my
petticoats and. . . ." She drew a long breath. "I warned
Papa not to try . . . I told him there wasn't anything he
could do against so many . . . even if he could get his
hands on the gun, he'd just get himself hurt, but when
they started pawing me and passing me from one to the
other to be mauled and kissed. . . They shot him when
he tried to interfere, shot him and clubbed him down
with a gunbarrel. It turned them mean and ugly. I don't
know what would have happened if a man hadn't come
riding into camp and told them angrily to get moving,
they had no business wasting time. . . . Well, yes," she
said a little stiffly, not looking at the men about her, "I
reckon I do know what would have happened, if he
hadn't come."

Jesse McAuliffe asked, "Would you recognize this
man, the one who gave the orders, if you saw him
again?"

She thought for a moment and shook her head doubt-
fully. "I . . . don't think so. It was dark, by that time;
and the minute those others let me go, I ran to Papa, of
course, and tried to stop the flow of blood. When I
looked up again, they'd all gone. They'd left our horses,
thank God. I . . . I managed to get Papa into the wagon.
I didn't stop for much of anything else; I just drove in
what I thought was the right direction, but I must have
got turned around in the dark, and then it rained. . . . It
seems like I've been soaking wet and driving in circles
for days!"

"Well, you're all right now, ma'am," Jesse McAuliffe
said. He studied her with a frown. "Most folks going to
Fort Gibson, as I recall, used to come in from the east,
taking a boat up the river at least as far as Fort Smith,
and sometimes clear to Gibson, water permitting."

The girl's eyes narrowed slightly. "What do you mean, Major McAuliffe?"

"Why," the Old Man said gently, "I was just wondering why a man with a pretty daughter, and business in Fort Gibson, would want to make the hard journey overland across Indian Territory, when they could have traveled so much more safely and comfortably by riverboat."

Chuck, annoyed with his father's attitude, found much to admire in the way the girl took it. She faced right up to the Old Man and laughed.

"You're a suspicious man, Major," she murmured. "I suppose you'll be even more suspicious of us, in that gray army coat of yours, after you've heard Papa talk. So I'll tell you right now, he talks like a Yankee because he is a Yankee; and there have been times when I've been ashamed of that, but I'm not any longer. Mama left him at the beginning of the war and took me back home to South Carolina. She . . . she died of lung fever, which she caught trying to save a few things the night Sherman's men burned our home in Columbia. After the war, Papa came looking for me. I didn't want to go with him, you understand—I hated everything he stood for; I'd been taught to—but there wasn't anything left and I had no place to go. He's been very kind. It wasn't until I thought he was dying that I realized how kind. . . ." Her voice broke. "You'll get him to a doctor at Fort Gibson as soon as possible? Please?"

The Old Man frowned again. "I'm afraid that's out of the question, Miss Netherton."

Her eyes widened. "Out of the question? Why?"

He said, "We're about two days north of the place already, and a couple of days east, as close as I can figure —we gave it a wide berth on purpose. Most of us have had quite enough dealings with the Union Army. . . . Anyway, I can't turn my herd around now. Nor can I spare you enough men for an adequate escort, considering the size of the gangs that seem to infest this part of the country."

"You'd let a man die because of your silly old cattle?" Her voice was sharp.

The Old Man looked down at her bleakly. "Miss Netherton," he said, "six or eight men, at least, have already died because of those silly old cattle. Two were from my own crew. One was my . . ." He checked himself, and went on in a different tone. "Anyway, I don't know how much of a force is maintained at Gibson these days, but I'm under the impression it's been greatly reduced. They may not even have a surgeon. You'll be sure of help at Baxter Springs, which is where we're headed. In the meantime, if you wish, I'll have a look at your father myself. I have some experience with bullet wounds."

She said angrily, "Don't trouble yourself!" Then her face crumpled into an expression close to tears, and she said breathlessly, "I'm sorry! Of course I want you to look! I . . . I'm just so . . . I don't mean to be unreasonable. Please forgive me!"

The Old Man bowed, and started towards the wagon, but paused to look at her. "You didn't say why your father chose to drive overland, Miss Netherton."

She said stiffly, "No, Major, I didn't. Why don't you ask him? I'm sure he had his reasons." She watched Jesse McAuliffe climb into the wagon; and swung on Chuck, standing nearby. "I declare, your daddy doesn't trust people much, does he?" she cried. "What does he suspect us of, smuggling guns and whiskey to the Indians?"

She broke off, as the Old Man stuck his head out again. He paid her no immediate attention. "Joe, take the men back to the herd," he said. "Keep it moving. We'll be along when we can. Chuck, you go with them. Bring me the black leather case from my warbag, and clean cloth for bandages, if you can find some. . . . Wait." He turned at last to the girl. "Miss Netherton, I want your permission to probe for the bullet. I am not a surgeon and I make no guarantees. All I will say is that I have done it before."

Amanda Netherton licked her lips. "Successfully, Major?"

The Old Man said calmly, "Both successfully and unsuccessfully."

"And if I don't give permission?"

"Then your father will certainly lose his leg, and probably his life."

"That leaves me little choice," she said quietly. "Go ahead. But . . ."

"Yes, Miss Netherton?"

She shook her head quickly. "No. I was going to say something foolish. Just go ahead."

"Very well," the Old Man said. "Now you'd better come in here. I'll need your help."

5.

THE WEATHER held fine as they moved northwards. This wasn't an unmixed blessing, Chuck discovered. When the ground dried, the dust came, and he had to eat plenty of it, riding in the drag of the herd. In the evenings, the Netherton wagon would pull up some distance from the main camp. The Old Man had laid down the law about that.

"This is a cattle drive," he'd said the first night after the girl and her father had joined them, "not a Sunday social. The young lady seems competent to handle her team without help, and if she can't cook or build a fire it's time she learned. She's been supplied with as much food as we can spare, and there's wood and water around for the taking. We've got a herd to look after. I can think of no good reason for any man from this outfit to hang around that wagon—or any boy, either," he'd finished, looking straight at Chuck.

There had been some laughter at this, the memory of which still rankled. Therefore, about the fourth night, when the Old Man came in from scouting the route of the next day's drive, and announced that he was going across to see his patient, and that Chuck could come along if he wished, Chuck made a point of showing no eagerness whatever. He took his time about getting his horse and mounting up. The Old Man was waiting.

"Kind of dusty back there today," he said, as they rode slowly towards the light of the Netherton fire.

"Yes, sir," Chuck said.

"It was proved during the war," the Old Man said deliberately, "that experience in the ranks never hurt an officer."

"No, sir," Chuck said.

"Anyway," the Old Man said, "somebody's got to look

after the remuda and ride in the drag. You can't run an outfit that's all trail bosses and top hands. . . ." It was, Chuck supposed, an explanation and apology of sorts, and his father was waiting for him to speak, but he could not think of what to say. Then the moment was past. The Old Man was talking again, looking towards the wagon ahead. "Just remember one thing," he was saying cryptically, "when you're young you bleed easily, but you heal quickly."

Chuck had no time to figure out what was meant by this, and the Old Man did not press the point, if he had one to make. A slender figure had come out of the Netherton wagon to greet them. Jesse McAuliffe reined in and looked down at the girl.

"In this country, ma'am," he said, "when you hear riders coming, don't go to meet them without a gun in your hands. How's your father?"

"Much better," she said. "We want to thank you—"

The Old Man said curtly, "I would not leave a dog to die out here, Miss Netherton." He glanced at Chuck. "Wait for me here."

He dismounted, strode to the wagon, and climbed inside. They heard him ask a question, in the same brusque voice, and they heard the sick man's reply. Amanda Netherton moved to the side of Chuck's horse and looked up.

"Aren't you going to get down, Mr. McAuliffe?"

He hesitated, and stepped down from the saddle. There was enough light from the fire so that he could see her clearly. Her face was clean now, and he'd been right about her being pretty—beautiful was the word that came unbidden into his mind. Her hair was put up neatly about her head. He wasn't sure that he hadn't liked it better loose and flowing. She was still wearing the same green traveling outfit, carefully brushed free of mud, but noticeably faded and stained by the hardships of the past week. He would not have thought of it as detracting from her appearance, however, except that she seemed embarrassed about its condition: she made a quick gesture of rubbing away a sooty smudge left by recent labors at the fire.

"Don't look at me so critically, Mr. McAuliffe," she said with a laugh. "I know I look positively shipwrecked. I've even had a notion to come over to your wagon and

borrow some clothes, if I'd thought you'd have some to
fit me."

She laughed again to show that she was joking. Of
course, no gently reared young lady would actually display herself in a man's trousers—or even mention the
garment by name. Even as a joke, the suggestion was quite
daring, and it brought an uneasy silence between them.

"Let me give you a cup of coffee," she said, and when
she'd poured it and given it to him: "From the lack of
company we've had, you'd think Papa was suffering from
plague instead of a simple bullet wound."

Chuck said uncomfortably, "It's the Old Man's orders,
ma'am. I reckon he figures all the men would be over
here if he'd let them. Probably he's right."

She smiled slowly. "Why, that was a real pretty speech,
Mr. McAuliffe. . . . They call you Chuck, don't they?
Does that mean your name is Charles?"

"Yes, ma'am."

"Mine is Amanda," she said.

"Yes, ma'am, I know."

"Your father doesn't seem to think very highly of us,"
she said, with a glance at the wagon. "Does he still suspect us of selling whiskey to the Indians?"

"Oh, I'm sure he doesn't think that, ma'am," Chuck
said quickly. "It's just . . . well, he's got his mind set on
getting these steers to market, and anything that threat-
ens to delay . . . Anyway, he hasn't exactly been sociable
towards anybody since Dave died."

"Dave?"

"My brother," Chuck said. "He was shot by those
bushwhackers that hit us at the Arkansas . . . the same
ones you ran into. Dave went through the war in the Old
Man's outfit; they were pretty close. . . ."

He stopped, as the wagon shook with movement, and
Jesse McAuliffe appeared. The Old Man went straight to
his horse, and Chuck made a move towards his own
mount, but his father paused to look at him.

"Don't stay too late," he said. "Nobody's going to take
your guard for you."

"No, sir," Chuck said.

"Good night, ma'am. I think you need have no more
worries about your father's health, as far as this wound's
concerned."

Jesse McAuliffe raised his hat towards Amanda, and rode away towards the light of the other fire. The girl stood looking after him, frowning.

"Now, whatever did he mean by that?" she murmured, with a glance at Chuck.

"By what?" Chuck asked, surprised.

The girl laughed. "Never mind. Let me fill your cup again."

"Yes, ma'am. It's better coffee than the cook makes—we call that six-shooter coffee." He explained diffidently: "Because it's thick enough to float a pistol, ma'am."

Her laugh was delighted and rewarding, and he found himself gaining confidence in her presence. Soon they were sitting near the fire, and he was talking to her as he'd talked to no one in years, not even Dave, whom he had been unable to trust not to make fun of him and call him Sonny if he said something naive. It came as a shock to discover, presently, that the fire had died to coals while he was rattling on about himself. He threw an uneasy glance up at the stars, and started to rise.

"I didn't realize . . ." he said, embarrassed. "It's almost time for me to go on guard."

She touched his arm. "No, please. Tell me more about your ranch. It sounds wonderful."

He said, "It was a real nice place before the war, but it's not much now, and it won't be ours much longer if we can't sell this herd for enough to pay the taxes."

"And you ran it by yourself, all through the war?"

He grimaced. "I've really been blowing my horn, haven't I, ma'am? It wasn't so much a question of running it as of keeping things from falling apart completely. And I wasn't alone; I managed to keep a crew of sorts, kids, and old men, and cripples. . . ."

"I should think your father would be very proud of you."

"Well," Chuck said dryly, "if he is, you sure can't tell by looking. . . . You haven't told me a thing about yourself, ma'am. Reckon I haven't given you much of a chance."

She laughed softly. "There's not much to tell, except that I'm a girl who's getting mighty fed up, right now, with harnessing horses and chopping wood. Oh, I learned to take care of myself after Mama died; I learned to do things I'd never dreamed I'd have to put my hand to. I was trained to be pretty and decorative and helpless; I can sew and embroider and play the piano. . . ."

"I'd like to hear you," Chuck said when she paused.

"You aren't likely to," she said, smiling. "Not out here. I don't suppose there's a piano within a hundred miles, and if there is, in Baxter Springs say, it's probably in a saloon or gambling house." She still had her hand on his arm. After a moment, she said, "I'd like you to do something for me, Chuck."

"Anything, ma'am."

She laughed softly. "Two things. One, please don't call me ma'am any more. And the second . . ." She hesitated, and went on: "The second is, I'd like you to kiss me, Chuck." He stared at her, shocked, and she continued quickly: "It would mean nothing, you understand, except that . . . well, I'm feeling lonely and bedraggled and unattractive, and it would help. It would help very much. You'd have to be a woman to understand how much."

He was still staring at her like a fool, feeling the light touch of her hand like fire on his arm, wanting to rise and flee, and not really wanting to, either. Then she leaned forward slightly, and suddenly he was holding her and kissing her clumsily, recalling the time, years ago, as a young boy, he'd kissed the little daughter of some visiting friends, experimentally. . . . it hadn't been so much, he remembered, nothing to make a fuss over. . . . But this was no little girl in his arms now, and he wasn't a young boy, either, and it was like suddenly being snatched away by a raging river in flood. Her hands were holding him fiercely, encouraging him, and he was fumbling with her clothing, half expecting lightning to strike him dead, and nothing of the sort happened. She didn't even protest or draw away, although what was happening no longer bore much relation to the innocent, meaningless kiss she'd asked him for. . . .

He panicked, losing courage and desire abruptly. What he'd been about to do, he realized, had been a shocking and despicable thing: he must have misunderstood. What he'd taken for encouragement must have been simple passive acceptance of the fate he'd been about to inflict upon her. She was a woman alone in a land of rough men, dependent upon them for protection; she'd simply not dared to resist him.

He found himself standing above her, guilty and ashamed. He tried to speak, but the words would not pass a sudden obstruction in his throat. He watched her rise and bring order to her garments, and walk forward to poke the fire with a piece of kindling. A flame sprang up. She dropped the kindling to feed it, and lifted her hands to her hair.

Without looking at him, she said, "You're very young, aren't you, Chuck?" He still could not speak, standing there abashed, and she turned deliberately to face him. "Don't feel badly," she said. "The fault was mine. As I told you, after Mama died, I learned to . . . to do things I never dreamed. . . . When you find a nice girl to marry, some day, you can tell her how you were almost seduced by a wicked woman out on the prairie, but you had the strength to resist . . . Chuck."

"Yes, ma'am." His voice obeyed him at last, but hoarsely.

"Tell your father, since he's so curious, that there will be a railroad to Fort Gibson within the next few years, as soon as the government decides to make the land available. Papa was hired to look over the possible routes for some interested speculators. That's why he didn't take a boat up the river. Naturally, we'd appreciate your not talking about it to anyone else. . . . And you can also tell your father, Chuck, that he'll never get this herd of his past Baxter Springs."

"Why not?" Chuck demanded.

"There have been outbreaks of Spanish fever among cattle all over the state of Kansas, wherever your Texas herds came through last year. The farmers are up in arms. There has been a quarantine law on the books since before the war. You must have heard about it."

"Yes, ma'am, but other outfits managed to slip through all right, so we figured—"

"Nobody's slipping through this year. The quarantine's being enforced to the hilt. If you try to drive on to Sedalia along this trail, you will be mobbed. Your only hope is to swing to the west and try to drive around the area of heavy settlement. I've heard that one or two herds did get through near a town called Jepson, well out along the state line. Remember the name, Jepson. Maybe you can slip across there." She regarded him for a moment longer. When she spoke again, there was tart-ness in her voice. "Now you'd better get back to your cows."

He hesitated, but there wasn't really anything left to be said, and he turned and stumbled to his horse. He climbed into the saddle.

"Chuck."

"Yes, ma'am," he said, looking down at her. He could not help noting that her dress, not fully fastened in front now, showed a hint of the white garments beneath, shaped to the roundness of her breasts. She caught the direction of his glance, smiled, and began to work with the small buttons, without haste.

"Good-bye, Chuck," she said. "And good luck."

He swung his horse around and fled, feeling depraved, foolish, and young.

6.

AMANDA NETHERTON smiled, watching the boy riding away at a gallop. He rode beautifully, she thought, like all these Texans. Of course, with their great clumsy saddles and ridiculous long stirrups, they had no real style, and if it ever came to jumping, they'd probably be disemboweled by their own saddle horns. But they were horsemen nevertheless; there was no doubt of that.

Standing there, she found herself remembering her glossy thoroughbred, called Prince, and how the groom would bring him around in the morning, and check the girth of the side-saddle; and there would, of course, always be a gentleman handy to hold the stirrup and help her up—generally, she recalled, a gentleman named Alan, who could be counted on to make some flattering remark about her appearance as they rode away together.

Well, Prince had been taken by the cavalry, and Alan had died in the swamp that was often referred to as The Wilderness, and she was standing by a dying fire in the middle of a dusty prairie with calloused hands and stringy hair, in grimy clothes she'd hardly had off for a week. Even Alan would be hard put to find something nice to say about her appearance now, she reflected ruefully.

At that, she was better off than she'd been at times

in the not too distant past, she reminded herself. She was neither starving nor freezing, and that was important. It had taken her a while, she reflected, but she'd learned her lesson well: the only truly important things in life were food, warmth, and money; and what you had to do to get them was really of very little consequence.

"Amanda." It was the voice of the man in the wagon. "Would you come here a moment, my dear?"

She shivered abruptly, and turned from the fire, slapping the dust from her skirts. He was sitting up when she climbed inside. The candle was out, but she could see the vague shape of him at the end of the limited space.

"I declare, you don't have to sound so disgustingly paternal," she said. "There's no one around to hear."

"Indeed?" he said. "I thought I heard him ride off, but then I decided my ears must have been deceiving me. You'd certainly never have let him leave so soon, if you'd had the say." He leaned forward and grasped her wrist. "What's the matter? Can't the aristocratic Miss Netherton even seduce a cowherd from Texas these days?"

"You're hurting me," she said evenly.

"I heard you," he said. "I heard you pumping the boy about his ranch and his cattle. Are you thinking of moving south, Miss Netherton? Are you thinking of leaving me for this juvenile *vaquero,* now that I'm flat on my back—like you left that young Army lieutenant for me when he got himself cashiered?"

"I didn't leave him!" she protested quickly. "I thought the fool had money of his own, I never dreamed he was stealing it! And I'd have stood by him if he'd wanted me to; if he hadn't showed so plainly that . . . that he was ashamed of me. Just as I'm standing by you now."

After a moment he released her wrist. "Well, see that you do, Mandy!"

"You'd be dead now if I hadn't," she pointed out.

He wasn't in a mood to be reminded of what he owed her. "Never mind that! Just remember, no woman runs out on Jack Keller!"

She glanced uneasily towards the opening behind her. "Don't say it so loud, you fool."

"I thought you said there was nobody around. Anyway, I don't flatter myself the name's known clear to

Texas—although some day it will be."

"Well, if you're Jack Keller, you can't very well be my nice Papa Netherton, can you?" she said reasonably. "It would raise questions, to say the least, if you were overheard. And the boy's gone, but the old man might have sent somebody over to spy on us. He suspects something, I know he does. Did he say anything when he was in here? What did he ask you?"

"Just medical questions. And he was kind of curious about the man who shot me, and how the shooting took place. . . ."

"If you'd taken my advice," she said, "there'd have been no shooting, and you wouldn't be lying there with a hole in your leg." She grimaced in the dark. "Silks and satins you promised me, as I recall, but the one nice dress you actually bought me, you've made me ruin driving miles through the rain to save you, and cooking beef and beans over a smoky fire to feed you!"

"Don't blame me for that!" he said irritably. "You didn't have to come running with nothing but the clothes on your back. If you'd taken time to make a few sensible preparations . . ."

"The Preacher wasn't waiting for me to make any preparations," she said angrily. "He was shaking like a leaf; the ride must have dried up all the whiskey inside him. He was in a fearful hurry to get back with the wagon; it was just an afterthought, his stopping for me. He wouldn't even let me buy bandages and medicines in town because somebody might ask questions. Actually, he just brought me along so he wouldn't have to stay with you himself, or try to make one of the others stay—not that there was much hope of that."

"They'd have stayed, if they were ordered to, if they knew what was good for them!"

"With you sick and out of your head? That riffraff?" she said. "Not likely! Their own skin comes first, with them."

"You're very clever at changing the subject six times a minute, Mandy," Keller said harshly. "But just remember this: if I ever catch you with a man, I'll kill him. So stay away from that young Texan, if you want him to live!"

She saw that he was really angry, really jealous, and it pleased her. When you could no longer make a man jealous, you'd lost your hold on him. But it was time to calm him down, before he started shouting at her loudly enough to be heard at the other camp, and she moved along the wagon bed until she was beside him.

"The boy is nothing to me," she said indifferently. "Kill him if you like." She ran her fingers down his bearded cheek, lightly, wondering why nature had given whiskers to man. Even if it was currently fashionable, she couldn't help thinking it was really rather repulsive, all that hair on the face. "And after you've shot him to death," she asked him softly, "what will you do to me?"

"Well," he said sullenly, "if I really thought there'd been something between you, I'd break you in two."

"It sounds downright thrilling," she murmured, lying close to him in the dark. Her mind was far away, as always under such circumstances. As a matter of fact, she was thinking of her first ball dress, pure and shining white, with hoops almost too wide to go through a door. "Break me, honey," she heard herself whispering, in the low throaty way that men seemed to find exciting. "Break me in two. . . ."

He moved towards her awkwardly, hampered by his wounded leg. It had been such a pretty dress, she thought, caressing him with a practiced simulation of passion. It had been such a pretty life, full of graciousness and beauty. Where had it gone? Where had it all gone?

7.

WHEN CHUCK reached camp, Joe Paris was waiting for him. He thought this meant he was going to catch hell for being late, and he was certain of it when Joe led him around the wagon to where the Old Man was sitting against a wheel, making notes in his journal by the light of the coal-oil lantern. But the Old Man merely glanced up, made a gesture to indicate that they were to sit, and continued writing. Presently he closed the journal, wrapped it carefully in oilskin, and laid it aside.

"Chuck," he said, looking up after a moment, "I owe you an apology."

"An apology, sir?"

"I brought you to the Netherton wagon this evening with ulterior motives. We'll be in Kansas shortly, maybe tomorrow, and I have a decision to make. Perhaps you can help me. Naturally, I will not ask you to reveal anything of a private nature that passed between you and the young lady—if anything did—but if she told you something you feel at liberty to repeat, I'd be obliged if you'd let me hear it."

Chuck was staring at his father incredulously. "You took me over there to . . . to spy on them?"

The Old Man shrugged his shoulders, showing more embarrassment than was his habit. "I have made it fairly clear that I do not trust those people. I have reasons, I might add. Perhaps I should have been more subtle. At any rate, knowing my attitude, they weren't likely to speak freely to me. I thought they might to you . . . one of them, at least." He drew a long breath. "Please believe me, Chuck, I am trying to be fair. I do not wish to act hastily. If Miss Netherton had something important to say, something in her own behalf, you'll be doing her a favor if you tell me."

Chuck struggled between bewilderment and anger. "You make it sound like . . . like a trial, sir!"

"You might call it that," the Old Man agreed.

Chuck glanced at Joe Paris, whose face was grim, and looked back at his father, and cried: "But I don't understand! What accusation . . . They've committed no crime!"

"I believe they have," Jesse McAuliffe said. "I believe that one of them is guilty of murder."

Chuck started to speak quickly, and stopped. The silence endured lengthily, broken at last by the sound of Pat Wills, the night guard, coming in from the herd and dismounting at the picket line. His partner, still out there, could be heard singing to the cattle in a low voice. The words were Spanish. Guiltily, Chuck glanced up at the stars and started to rise.

His father said, "I've spoken to Miguel. He'll stay on guard a little longer tonight. You can relieve him early tomorrow."

Chuck nodded mechanically. "Murder?" he whispered.

"It's a serious charge," the Old Man said. "That's why I want any information you can give me. I want to make no mistake."

"Aren't you going to give them a chance to speak in their own defense?"

"They'll have that opportunity, of course." The Old Man looked at him hard. "However, it's my feeling that the speech for the defense has already been made. That's a clever young woman. She wouldn't pass up the opportunity to tell her story to receptive ears. What did she say, Chuck?"

Chuck hesitated, feeling trapped and helpless and furiously angry at the way he seemed to have been used by everyone tonight. Joe Paris leaned forward.

"Come on, boy. If it's the young lady you're worrying about, you know the Major won't hurt her; we don't fight women. Anyway, it's the man we want."

"Her father?"

Joe laughed. "Maybe he is that, but I wouldn't bank on it."

Chuck looked at him in horror and disbelief. Jesse McAuliffe said quickly: "The relationship between them isn't a matter of importance. The man may well be her father, which would excuse her actions to a great extent—but not his."

He stopped there, and the two older men sat in silence, watching Chuck and waiting for him to speak. He could feel the pressure of their regard, and he knew that it was important for him to think clearly, but his mind was a confused jumble of thoughts and images.

"She said—" He had to clear his throat and start over. "She said you'd never get this herd past Baxter Springs."

"Indeed?" The Old Man's voice was gentle. "Why not?"

"Because of the quarantine—"

Joe Paris said impatiently, "We know all about their quarantine. They've had it for years, but they've never done much about it."

The Old Man waved him into silence. "It's possible that the girl, having recently come from the north, has better information than we have. What else did she say, Chuck?"

"The quarantine is being enforced this year, to the hilt, she said. If we try to drive to Sedalia, we'll be mobbed. There's only one place where we maybe can slip through, a town to the west called Jepson—"

"Ah, never mind all that!" Joe said. "Did she have a

story to explain what she and this man were doing here in the Nations?"

"She said—" Chuck licked his lips. "She said there's going to be a railroad built to Fort Gibson, and some speculators had hired her father to make a survey—"

"A railroad!" Joe snorted. "You're sure he wasn't digging a canal across the prairie, instead?"

The Old Man said reprovingly, "It's not unlikely that a railroad will be built here some day, Joe, maybe even clear to Texas. However, I doubt that the man in that wagon knows a transit from a chain. The young woman went a little far out of her way to explain how he came to lose his instruments, and she her clothes; I doubt they ever had any along. Chuck, that story isn't good enough without proof. Is that all she told you?"

"Yes, sir, but—"

Jesse McAuliffe said, "I'm not being as arbitrary and unreasonable as you seem to think. I've had my suspicions from the beginning; it was just a little too pat, meeting them where we did. But there was no hurry, and I wanted to be sure. Tonight, finally, I got the man to tell me exactly how he's supposed to've been shot. He says that, when these alleged ruffians began to abuse his daughter, he picked up a heavy stick and started to her aid. A man from the group rose to meet him, drew a pistol, shot him in the leg, and clubbed him to the ground when he did not fall immediately—"

"But that's exactly what Amanda . . . what Miss Netherton told us!"

The Old Man shook his head. "You don't understand. I had to have the details, to be sure they were lying. Chuck, I extracted the bullet, remember? When one standing man shoots another in the leg, it's hardly possible for the bullet to strike above the knee and range *upwards* into the thigh."

"On the other hand," Joe Paris interjected, "it's just the kind of wound a man on horseback might get, being shot by another rider at point-blank range—particularly if the shooting happened so fast the second rider never had time to raise his pistol, but fired from the hip."

"There were grains of powder in the wound," the Old Man said. "Your brother's gun was fully discharged when he was found, but he wasn't one to go riding around with an empty pistol in his fist. He'd been trained, in a

fight, to hold back one load for a real emergency. Well,
it came, I believe: a horseman charging out of the dust
and darkness right on top of him. I see both men firing
simultaneously, both riding on a little ways to fall from
the saddle gravely wounded, in one case mortally
wounded. . . ." The Old Man's voice stopped.

"Dave?" Chuck whispered. "You think Mr. Netherton
killed *Dave?*"

8.

SITTING THERE, with his own words still sounding in
his ears, Chuck could hear the deep, hoarse voice of
Sam Biederman, who'd joined Miguel on guard, singing
to the cattle in incomprehensible, guttural German that
sounded like a savage chant. Chuck thought of a wooden
cross in the rain, and of a woman's warm lips and
strong, small hands. . . . He'd told her about Dave, he
recalled. She'd seemed only mildly interested, with no
more than the sympathetic concern anybody would display, hearing of someone else's bereavement. She'd
asked him to kiss her, and permitted him—led him—to
go much further. Well, he reflected wryly, if you were
going to be a damn fool, you might as well be a big damn
fool, it cost no more.

Joe Paris was speaking. "Dave brought a nice pair of
Remingtons back from the war," the foreman said. "He
didn't figure to need two guns in peacetime, and he didn't
have a present for his kid brother, anyway, so he split
the pair. He gave one to you, and loose powder and
round balls to fit it; but he saved his small supply of
paper cartridges for himself, with the long, heavy conical
bullets." Joe reached into his shirt pocket. "Here's the
bullet the Major dug out of Netherton, if that's his
name. It's battered some, but if you cut the lead from
one of those cartridges of Dave's I gave you the other
day, and compare the two, I think you'll find they're the
same caliber and even the same shape. It would be a
real coincidence, out here on the border, finding two .44
caliber long bullets from different sources cast from
molds so similar."

The Old Man's voice said quietly, "I think the evidence is fairly conclusive, Chuck."

"But—" Chuck had difficulty speaking the name. "But Miss Netherton. How do you account for her presence. Surely you don't think she was riding with the gang—"

The Old Man said, "We spent almost a week, what with hunting strays, coming less than thirty miles from the river—plenty of time for a man on a good horse to reach the settlements, pick up the lady and a team and wagon, and drive back to where the wounded man was waiting."

"But if he was one of the outfit that jumped us, wouldn't his friends stay—"

"Varmints like that have no friends," Joe Paris said harshly. "I'm surprised they even went as far as they did in looking after him. It would seem to indicate that he's somebody important among them, maybe even their leader. Otherwise, I'd have expected them just to leave him behind to die."

The Old Man said, "They left him in the care of the girl. Whether she then, driving towards the settlements, ran into us by accident, or whether, when her man's condition grew worse, she took the desperate gamble of approaching us for help deliberately, only she can tell us." He grimaced. "I would say the latter. She was a little too obviously a maiden in distress, a little too artfully muddied and disheveled, and her accent was a little too obviously designed to appeal to Texas ears. . . . A resourceful young woman. I think it's time we paid her another visit." Jesse McAuliffe regarded his son for a moment. "You can wait here if you like. Joe and I will do what is necessary."

Chuck licked his dry lips. "What are you planning, sir?"

"Miss Netherton will be free to go," the Old Man said. "She is, at most, an accomplice after the fact, and as Joe says, we don't fight women. Unless the man can explain away the evidence against him, we'll hang him."

Chuck said, "The law—"

"This is Indian Territory, boy. The only law here, as far as I know, is the Union Army, and if our experience with occupation troops is any guide, they won't consider shooting an ex-rebel a serious offense. As for taking him on to Kansas and turning him over to the autho-

rities there, I don't intend to leave his punishment to the
whims of a Yankee judge and jury." He paused, and went
on: "It's not entirely a personal matter. There'll be other
herds following us. We may be coming this way ourselves next year. We've got to teach this border scum
that it doesn't pay to molest a Texas outfit."

The Old Man raised the glass of the lantern and blew
out the flame. Then he rose, tall in the darkness, took
his gunbelt from where it hung over a spoke of the
wagon wheel, and buckled it on. There was a purposeful
grimness about him. He was a just and law-abiding man
in his way, but he came from a race that had never taken
much stock in the biblical injunction about turning the
other cheek.

Joe Paris got to his feet, lifted his revolver from the
holster, spun the cylinder experimentally, and replaced
the weapon. Chuck got up, as the two older men started
to leave.

"Sir?"

"Yes, Chuck."

"If you're right, it's more or less a family affair, and
I'd better have a hand in it, hadn't I?"

"I hoped you would see it that way," the Old Man
said, and nothing more.

Mounted, they started away from camp, but reined
in as Miguel Apodaca rode up. The little Mexican
vaquero looked at the three of them before speaking.

"Will you need help, *señor*?" he asked Jesse Mc-
Auliffe. "Should I wake the others?"

"Not for a girl and a man with a bad leg."

"I have been watching, as you asked. A little while
ago the *señorita* built up the fire again, it was almost
out. Now it burns brightly, as you can see, but they are
both in the wagon; I have not seen them again."

"Thanks, Miguel."

"Be careful, *señor*. A man with a bad leg is nothing,
but a woman with a double-barreled shotgun, that can be
formidable."

Miguel spun his horse about and cantered back towards the herd. The Old Man made a gesture, and they
rode towards the yellow, flickering fire, not too far away.
Beyond it, the wagon sheet shone dimly white. Chuck
found himself wondering unhappily what it would be like
to hang a man—with the girl, daughter or mistress or

whatever she might be, looking on. It wasn't anything like galloping towards the muzzles of hostile rifles and returning their fire. . . .

"Major!" It was Joe's voice, sharp and perturbed. Jesse McAuliffe said, "Yes, I see it. . . . As I said, a resourceful young woman."

Chuck said, "What—"

Then he saw it, too: the fire burning brightly before a canvas carefully draped over bushes and supported by sticks to simulate the cover of a wagon. At a distance, in the dark, the illusion had been perfect.

Joe swore bitterly. "They can't have gone far!"

"Even so, it'll be hard to trail them at night without a moon. She undoubtedly counted on that," Jesse McAuliffe said. "We'll wait until daylight. . . . Chuck?"

"Yes, sir."

"What was that town she mentioned?"

"Jepson," Chuck said.

"Jepson, eh. I wonder," the Old Man said thoughtfully, "why she went out of her way to call attention to the name. I have a feeling that young lady does very little without good reason." He sighed. "It is too bad—"

"What, sir?"

"She obviously came from people of quality. It is too bad she should find it necessary to consort with outlaws and murderers. Well, war is never kind to the defeated."

9.

IN THE MORNING, the Nethertons' camp-fire had burned itself out, but the ashes still sent a thin wisp of smoke skywards when Chuck and his father rode by. They paused briefly to look back at the herd, already in motion. Joe Paris, at the point, flung up an arm to wish them well. The Old Man acknowledged the signal.

"Shouldn't be much trouble tracking them," Chuck said, pointing to the plain marks left by wagon wheels in the soft ground.

"No," said the Old Man, "which makes me wonder just what they had in mind. They must have known they couldn't outrun us, even with several hours' start. And it seems hardly likely that the leader of a band of bush-whackers would dare take shelter in the settlements, un-less . . ."

"Unless what, sir?"

The Old Man shook his head. "We'll see," he said, set-ting off along the trial at a fast lope.

The fugitives had made no effort to cover their tracks, and Chuck and his father made good progress. The hunt had a kind of irresistible excitement about it, even though what lay at the end of it wouldn't be pleasant, and Chuck found himself absorbed in the sign on the ground to the extent that, when his father, in the lead, threw up his arm to signal a halt, it came as a shock to look up and find the trail ahead blocked by a crowd of armed men, afoot and on horseback. There were even several wagons, although not the one they sought.

It was a motley group, Chuck saw as he rode forward slowly beside Jesse McAuliffe: farmers in overalls, bearded ruffians wearing remnants of blue uniforms, even a few townsmen in sober, dark suits—they must be closer to Baxter than he'd thought, Chuck reflected. They bore weapons ranging from shotguns to long muskets of war-time origin, not to mention a sprinkling of the short, ugly Sharps carbines that, supplied to these areas before the war by the abolitionists under the urging of that emi-nent divine, Henry Ward Beecher, had come to be known as Beecher's Bibles. Trust a Yankee man of God, Chuck reflected bitterly, to go passing out rifles for the purpose of breaking the laws of both man and God.

A stout man rode forward to meet them, on a horse that would have looked better between the shafts of a plow.

"That's far enough," he said. He pulled back his coat so they could see the badge on his shirt. "This trail is closed."

"We're hunting a murderer," the Old Man said. He pointed to the tire tracks on the ground. "He came this way."

"A murderer, eh?" the sheriff said. "You wouldn't be referring to a young lady and her pa who came through town early this morning."

"There was a woman with him," the Old Man acknowl-edged.

"You're damn right there was a woman with him!" the stout man said. "As pleasant a young lady as ever I laid eyes on, and if she'd been willing to prefer charges, I'd be putting you under arrest this minute. We don't stand for abusing women around here, Mister!"

Chuck started to speak angrily, but his father silenced him with a gesture. "Arrest?" the Old Man said quietly. "What for?"

"You think it's lawful to detain people against their will, Mister? She told us all about it, how you fine chivalrous Texans kept her and her sick pa virtual prisoners for days. She put up with it, she said, for her pa's sake—he wasn't fit to travel fast—until she couldn't bear the indecent advances to which she was subjected and lit out in the middle of the night for help."

The Old Man said, "Well, I was brought up never to contradict a lady, Sheriff, but just why were we supposed to have detained her?"

"Why?" the fat man said. "So she couldn't drive ahead and warn us how you were planning to slip your herd of diseased longhorns past the quarantine, of course!" He turned his head to spit on the ground. "Now, I've got no real jurisdiction here, Mister, but I'm speaking for these citizens of Kansas when I tell you we don't want any of your wild Spanish stock even coming close to our state line, which is back only a couple of miles. This is plenty close enough. So ride back to your herd, Mister, and turn it around. Any animal that comes within range, we'll shoot it down."

There was a murmur of assent from the men behind him. The Old Man regarded them for a moment, and turned his attention back to the sheriff.

"Just as a matter of record, Sheriff," he said mildly, "I am telling you that the man who calls himself Netherton is a murderer and a member—perhaps even the leader—of a gang which attacked us a couple of weeks back, probably the same gang that wiped out the Laughlin outfit of twelve men last year, shooting them down in cold blood."

"A murderer, eh?" The stout man regarded him coldly. "My son died at Pittsburgh Landing, Reb. Maybe you were there, with that gray coat. Don't you go telling me about murderers! Now get along back and turn those cattle."

Chuck opened his mouth again, indignantly, but his father's hand was on his arm, restraining him. The Old Man picked up the reins and swung his pony around. Chuck followed. They rode away. It gave Chuck an uneasy feeling to turn his back on all those weapons, but the Old Man never looked around, so he didn't either.

Presently, Chuck heard his father make a small sound, and glanced that way warily. Probably the Old Man was bursting with fury, mild though his manner had been. You couldn't always tell. The Old Man wasn't one to rant and swear. He'd act smooth and polite until people got to thinking nothing would rile him; and then he'd go killing mad all in an instant.

The little sound came again. Chuck frowned, and looked more closely, shocked. His father was laughing heartily, almost silently.

"Indecent advances, eh?" the Old Man murmured.

Chuck felt his face go hot and his ears turn red. He tried to say something, but couldn't. Then the Old Man reached out and clapped him on the knee without speaking, and they rode on in silence, father and son.

10.

THEY TURNED the herd westward. There was some discussion of turning east, bypassing Kansas in that direction, but other herds had tried that route in previous years, and stories of their hardships in the flint hills of Missouri had filtered back to Texas. Better to go a little farther and keep the cattle in good condition, than to reach market with a herd of sorefooted ambulating skeletons.

The following evening a little man came riding into camp on a fine tall bay that had a thoroughbred look. The rider was well dressed, but he wasn't much of a horseman; it was a good thing there wasn't much weight to him, Chuck thought, or that fine horse would have had a mighty sore back, the way he bounced around in the saddle. He asked for the man in charge and was invited to partake of food and coffee while he waited for the Old Man to return from his nightly scout. He ac-

cepted the coffee but refused the food—after a shocked
look at the evening's greasy stew—which didn't endear
him to the cook, or to anybody else in the outfit, for that
matter. It was all very well for them to complain about
the fare, but for a stranger to spurn it was an insult to
everybody.

Presently the Old Man came riding in, and the two of
them went around behind the wagon, the little man talking while the Old Man ate his supper. Chuck couldn't hear
what was being said, and he didn't want to seem to be
eavesdropping, so he busied himself wiping off his pistol
and fixing his bedroll for the night, but he was thoroughly aware when the Old Man came back into sight with
his empty tin plate and cup, to toss the plate into the
cook's pan of water and fill the cup with fresh coffee.
The little man was following him with the impatient,
frustrated look of one who'd talked himself out against
another man's silence.

"Well, Major McAuliffe?" he demanded.

The Old Man looked down at him and spoke deliberately: "Before I sell these cattle at your price, sir, I'll
slaughter them for their hides. Good day."

The little man started to speak angrily, but checked
himself. He strode to his handsome horse, reached the
saddle after three tries, and rode off with his coat-tails
flapping. That night, half a dozen unidentified riders tried
to stampede the herd, but the Old Man had the whole
crew awake and the attackers were driven off without
damage.

The next day, and the day after that, they moved
westward. On the morning of the fourth day they turned
north again, crossed the Kansas line—as near as they
could figure—and, on the following morning made some
six miles before they were stopped by grim men bearing
shotguns and pitchforks, accompanied by an officer of the
law who threatened to throw them all in jail and confis-
cate the cattle if they weren't out of the state by night-
fall. That evening, an unctuous personage who had the
look of a banker drove up in a shabby buggy that had
the look of a livery-stable rig and offered to buy the
herd at two dollars a head, saying that he was a kindly
man who couldn't bear to think of their having come all
the way from Texas for nothing. The Old Man threw him
out.

Back in Indian Territory, they continued to the west.
They had a week of good weather, but nobody appreciated it much, heading in the wrong direction. Tempers
grew strained; even the Old Man grew snappish and sarcastic, like he'd been right after his return from the war.
One evening he came riding into camp after being gone
most of the day, and summoned Chuck and Joe Paris to
him.

"Well, there it is," he said with a jerk of his head,
after tasting his coffee and spitting it out. "Coosie, for
the love of God," he said turning his head, "why don't
you wash your dishrag in the other pot?"

The cook came hurrying to take the cup and refill it,
something he'd have done for no one else in the crew.

When he was gone, Chuck asked, "What's there, sir?"

"Jepson, Kansas, of course. The town your lady friend
was so careful to impress upon your memory!"

Chuck flushed and was silent. Joe Paris asked, "How
far?"

"Just across the line, near as I can figure, about a
day's drive west."

Joe said, "We'd better give the place a wide berth.
We're not apt to find anything pleasant, following that
young female's advice."

"No," the Old Man said, "but we might find a murderer."

There was a little silence. Jesse McAuliffe's voice was
grim; there was no laughter left in him now, Chuck saw.
The past days of moving steadily away from their original destination, Sedalia, of butting repeatedly against
that wall of armed hostility to the north, had taken their
toll. There was the land of plenty, where cattle sold for
twenty and thirty dollars a head, almost within reach,
but always the way was barred.

"You think they'll be there?" Joe asked.

Jesse McAuliffe moved his shoulders. "If they are,
we'll have gained at least that much. If they aren't . . .
Maybe there was some good in the girl, after all. Maybe
she'd actually heard something and was giving us the
benefit of it, in return for our having saved her man's
life. I put no real faith in it, but it's worth a try. We
aren't getting any closer to the railroad this way, that's
for sure."

"I don't like it," Joe said.

"Neither do I," the Old Man said. "But I don't like driving these cattle clear to Colorado, either."

In the morning, they swung somewhat to the north, angling closer to the invisible line that marked the limit of Indian Territory. They drove all that day through open country with good grass and water. The longhorns were putting on weight, Chuck reflected; they'd be in fine shape to sell, if somebody was ever found to buy at a fair price.

They camped for the night by a small creek. In the morning they turned due north, moving into Kansas again. About noon, the Old Man, scouting ahead, came back into sight. As he approached he gave the signal to halt, while the low rise of ground behind him began to fill with men, more than they'd met anywhere before.

The Old Man's face was bleak when he reached them. "It's the same damn story," he said. "There's a young deputy sheriff back there says we've got to turn them around. Turn them and get them moving, he says, before he arrests the lot of us and impounds the herd."

"Moving's fine," Chuck said bitterly. "Did he happen to say where?"

His father shrugged. "Back into the Nations, I reckon. He said the local settlers have lost some stock to Spanish fever, and they don't aim to let us infect any more with our diseased animals."

Chuck felt impotent rage grip at his throat and chest. "Diseased?" He looked towards the men on the ridge, and heard their jeering laughter. "I'd like to see a couple of those cackling sod-busters come down here on foot. These poor diseased longhorns would soon make them laugh on the other side of their . . ."

He stopped, because his father wasn't listening. He was regarding the herd, with an odd faraway look that made Chuck uneasy. He seemed to be debating something with himself. Deliberately, he dropped the tied-together bridle reins, removed his hat and hung it on the saddle horn, and wiped his forehead with a bandana handkerchief, performing each act in order with his single hand. Then he returned the handkerchief to his pocket and, still frowning at his cattle, put the hat back on his head, lost in thought.

Suddenly he looked up. Chuck followed the direction of his father's glance, and saw that a large young man

with a badge on his shirt was riding down the shope towards them—that would be the deputy the Old Man had
mentioned. He was mounted on a big, awkward-looking
gray. With him was another man, also mounted, if you
could call it that. Some of these Yankees, Chuck reflected, didn't seem to care much what they put under
their saddles. Well, it wasn't hard to understand, when
you looked at the saddles. The two men reined in half a
dozen yards away.

"The boys are getting impatient," said the big young
deputy, not much older than Chuck himself. He had the
swaggering look some men got when you pinned a badge
on them, and he wore a fine new revolver at his hip.
"Your time's about up, McAuliffe," he said. "What's it
to be?"

Chuck heard his father draw a long, defeated breath.
"We'll move 'em," Jesse McAuliffe said. "How far does
this quarantine of yours run, anyway? Any way of getting clear around it?"

It was the other man who answered. "Not and reach
the railroad, there isn't, friend."

The Old Man turned a strangely mild glance on this
one, a long thin man in a shabby black suit and hat,
whose eyes were hidden by the reflections of gold-rimmed
spectacles. In contrast to his respectable clothes, his
breath, even at a distance, carried the aroma of strong
spirits.

"Who are you?" Jesse McAuliffe asked.

The deputy said, "This is Mr. Paine. He's got a proposition for you."

"So?" The Old Man didn't take his eyes from the thin
one. "Well, Mr. Paine?"

The man called Paine cleared his throat. It was long
enough and knobby enough, Chuck thought, to take a
bit of clearing; and the stiff collar surrounding it was
far from clean. Paine said: "You won't get this herd to
Sedalia, friend, or any other point on the railroad. The
quarantine line runs west of all of them. Oh, some of
you Texans slipped through last year, and even a few this
spring, but our good people are still paying the price in
dead and ailing cattle. They're not going to let it happen
again; they're ready to take to arms to prevent it, as you
can see."

The deputy nodded agreement. "As far as this county's concerned, the sheriff's given orders not to let a single head of Texas beef across the line. And I know the neighboring counties feel the same way."

"I see," the Old Man said. "You got any suggestions, friend?" He was still regarding the thin one steadily.

It was the deputy who spoke again, however, looking sourly at the nearest steer, tall and leggy, with a five-foot horn spread. "You call that a domestic animal?" he sneered. "As far as I'm concerned, you can take them all back to Texas, Mister. We don't want them here."

The thin man with the eyeglasses said quickly, "However, there's a reasonable solution to your problem, Major. It just happens that I have a contract to supply beef to a couple of Army posts to the west, outside the quarantine area. I'll take this herd off your hands, if the price is right."

Chuck saw his father's eyes narrow. "And your idea of a suitable price, sir?"

There was a little pause. Paine looked at Jesse McAuliffe and raised his head to let his small, veined eyes, behind the spectacles, sweep the herd appraisingly. "They've come a long ways. I'd have to fatten them up a bit before the Army'd take them. Three dollars."

Jesse McAuliffe's voice was soft and lazy. "Three dollars a head, sir, or three dollars for the entire herd?"

Paine flushed at the sarcasm. "Three dollars a head is my offer. . . . Yes, yes, friend, I know they're paying around twenty at the railroad, but the Army won't pay me that, and you're not at the railroad. Nor are you likely to get there. Think it over, friend, but don't think too long. Yours isn't the only herd that's been turned back. I wouldn't have to ride very far to find half a dozen Texas outfits marking time below the line, hoping for the quarantine to be lifted. Well, it won't be. . . . I suggest you return to the creek where you camped last night. I'll be over tomorrow morning for your answer. Come on, Reese."

Chuck watched the two men ride away. Their horsemanship, he decided, was just about up to the standard set by their saddles and horseflesh. He didn't want to look at his father and see that look of defeat in the Old Man's eyes. It had been there right after the war, he remembered, but it had faded gradually. Now it was back.

II.

JESSIE MCAULIFFE rubbed the stump of his left arm absently. He was staring towards the men on the rise.

"Chuck," he said quietly, "your eyes are younger than mine, boy. Look to the right. See anyone you know?"

Chuck stared at the silhouetted figures. He frowned abruptly, seeing a bearded figure on horseback a little to the rear.

"Why," he said, "it looks like Mr. Netherton . . ."

But his father had already swung his pony around, and was riding southwards along the edge of the herd. Chuck rode after him; and Joe Paris and the other riders, sensing that something was up, left their posts to converge upon the two of them. Jesse McAuliffe looked back once, as if to orient himself, at the noisy jeering crowd waiting on the brow of the rise. He rode until he had the herd squarely between himself and their position. Then he pulled up and let the crew gather about him.

He said to Joe Paris: "See him?"

Joe nodded. "The man must be tough. I didn't think he'd be in shape to ride yet."

The Old Man said, "Boys, those Yanks are getting real impatient for us to move." He looked hard at the little group of riders about him. Chuck saw that his father's pale blue eyes were suddenly very bleak and bright in his weathered face, stubbled with gray-white beard after the long weeks on the trail. Jesse McAuliffe reached down and pulled the Colt revolving pistol from its holster at his hip. "Let us oblige the gentlemen," he said softly. "Let us move these here diseased three-dollar cattle!"

Chuck, not quite comprehending his father's meaning, looked at the other men. He saw the sudden hard, bright look of excitement in their faces. It was the look of men just a little too familiar with lost causes; of men, like his father, turned a little mad by the sting of everlasting defeat.

Jesse McAuliffe's big pistol swung up and fired at the sky. Joe Paris laughed suddenly and whipped out his revolver and pulled the trigger. Somebody howled like a wolf, and the herd broke. One moment, the longhorns were still standing there, wary but motionless; the next moment they were off with a sound like sudden thunder, with the crew after them, fanning out to guide them and urge them along. Chuck caught sight of his father's gray coat disappearing into the dust downwind of the herd. He sent his pony after it, drawing the cap-and-ball Remington. The dust enveloped him.

He heard a gunshot ahead, dim above the sound of the stampeding cattle. Somewhere close by in the dust, Joe Paris howled like a coyote baying at the moon—for all his dry, middle-aged look, there was a streak of wildness in the man. The coyote-howl was answered by the high and quavering rebel yell from up ahead: that was the Old Man himself cutting loose. The excitement was contagious: Chuck raised his pistol and fired at the sky.

"Run, you Texas jackrabbits!" he yelled at the steers looming out of the dust on his left. "You've been craving it, now run your fool heads off!"

He felt his pony begin to labor as the ground rose before them. Then he was out of the dust again, close behind his father, with Joe Paris pulling alongside to the right. Ahead was the mob, what was left of it. Most of the Kansans were scrambling for safety, but a couple still stood staring in petrified disbelief at the onrushing river of longhorned cattle. Then these men, too, broke and ran. As the stampede rolled over the deserted crest of the hill, a shot sounded from the right and behind, and Jesse McAuliffe dropped his revolver and went slack in the saddle.

Chuck threw a glance over his shoulder. The big deputy sheriff was there, riding in at an angle on his clumsy gray. His face was contorted with anger, and he had his fine new revolver in his hand; but one shot was all the plug intended to stand for, and the deputy was having his hands full.

Ahead, Joe Paris had raced alongside the Old Man, whose coat was already dark and wet from the shoulder-blade down. Chuck heard a bullet go overhead, whether aimed at him or the older men ahead, there was no telling. He reined his pony around sharply, but the dust closed in again, and he could see no target. Then the

big gray, terrified by the shooting, running wild and uncontrollable, came charging out of the murk right on top
of him, and horses and men went down together.
Rolling free of the tangle, Chuck came to his feet.
He found that he still had his revolver in his hand. The
deputy was crawling around on hands and knees, scratching at the ground dazedly: Chuck realized that he
was groping for his own gun, which was nowhere to
be seen. Chuck raised his weapon, but the sights kept
blurring in a strange way, and he realized that blood
was running down his face and his head felt very strange.
He got a bead on the crawling figure of the other man,
and waited for the deputy to look around; somehow he
couldn't bring himself to fire at a man who wasn't
looking. But the deputy kept crawling the other way,
and Chuck couldn't be bothered with him any more. He
shoved the pistol into its holster, turned, and stumbled
through the dust to where Joe Paris was kneeling beside
a figure on the ground.
As Chuck came up, Joe rose, his face saying everything
that needed to be said. Chuck dropped heavily to his
knees beside the Old Man, who opened his eyes. His
lips moved.
"Sorry, boy," Jesse McAuliffe whispered. "Man should
never put off . . . Wanted to talk . . . tell you . . . thought
we'd have more time . . . later . . . Never enough time,"
he whispered. "Never enough time. . . ."
After a little, Chuck started to rise, but the world
was rotating strangely about him, and the day seemed
to be growing dark. He felt Joe Paris catch him as he
started to pitch forward across his father's body.

12.

HE AWOKE in bed, with a throbbing headache. When he
opened his eyes, he found the light painful, and quickly
closed them again, but not before discovering that he was
in a room with flowered wallpaper, smooth and clean,
and crisp white curtains at the windows. It had been a
long time since he'd seen anything of the sort.
Somebody left the room and said, outside the door,

"He's awake now, Dad." It was the voice of a girl or
young woman. He'd never heard it before.

A man answered her out there: "All right, honey."

Booted feet came through the door and approached
the bed. Chuck opened his eyes again, and looked up at
the man standing over him—a compact, grayhaired in-
dividual of indeterminate age. He had the leathery, dur-
able look that long exposure to the elements gives some
men. Once they get it, around the age of thirty-five or
forty, they don't change much until they die. This man
had gray eyes and a drooping gray mustache that partly
hid his mouth. He wore a badge on his shirt.

"I'm George Kincaid," he said. "I'm sheriff here. How
do you feel, McAuliffe?"

Chuck licked his lips. It was an effort to speak. "Don't
seem to be any pieces missing."

The grayhaired man smiled briefly. "Guess it's like the
Doc said after looking you over: you can't kill a Texan
by kicking him in the head, not even when it's a horse
does the kicking." His smile died. When he spoke again,
his voice was crisp. "How do you like your bad news,
son, short or long?"

Chuck looked at him for a moment. "Short," he
whispered.

"Your pa's dead."

He'd known it, of course, but it was a shock to hear it
in words, nevertheless. He had a moment of pure grief;
then bitterness and anger went through him like fire.

He whispered, "Got to hand it to you Yankees! It took
you a while, but you finally got him, didn't you?"

The man above him made a quick gesture. "Ah, don't
start that, boy! Nobody in these parts is fighting the war
any longer."

Chuck laughed. It hurt his head, but rage was hot
inside him, and he pushed himself up in the bed. His
voice came strongly now: "I sure appreciate your telling
me, sir. I was kind of beginning to have my doubts, what
with the bushwhackers, mobs, blockades, and quaran-
tines we've been running into, just trying to find a place
to sell a few head of cattle at a fair price. . . . Yes, sir, I
certainly am glad to hear you say that, Sheriff."

Kincaid said gently, "I'm making allowances for your
feelings, but don't get too sarcastic with me, young fellow."

Chuck stared at him grimly. "A bullet's a bullet, and dead's dead. The only difference is, your Yankee army never got a shot at the Old Man's back. It took a civilian with a badge to manage that!"

Kincaid winced and was silent briefly. Then he said grudgingly, "Granted that my deputy was a little hasty—"

"Hasty?" Chuck laughed again, harshly. "Sheriff, you do your man an injustice! Not hasty, not that one. He's a real careful gent. Oh, he's got his faults—he's not what you'd call the best horseman in the world—but hasty's not one of them. He's right cool and deliberate about his murdering, your Mr. Reese is!"

The sheriff shook his head. "I wouldn't talk like that around town, if I were you, McAuliffe. There's considerable feeling against you men already. You're lucky nobody was badly trampled or gored by those wild Spanish cattle of yours, but several citizens present lost some skin and all lost a good deal of dignity, the way I heard it. . . . Personallly, I'd have liked it better if Will Reese had kept his pistol holstered, and I've told him so; but he had plenty of provocation, and you won't find many folks around here blaming him for what he did. In fact, when they brought you fellows in here this afternoon, there was a good deal of sentiment in town for finishing the job by stringing up the lot of you." The sheriff paused, and went on: "You don't have to worry. They're cooling off, and I'm not in the habit of letting my prisoners be lynched, in any case."

"Prisoners?" Chuck murmured.

"What did you expect, son, after what you fellows tried to pull out there? You're under arrest. The rest of your outfit's in jail, but you can stay on here until the trial tomorrow. I don't figure you'll be going anywhere with that head; besides, you don't look like the kind to run out on your crew."

Chuck thought this over. "What about the cook and the wrangler?" he asked. "They had nothing to do with it."

"In that case, they've nothing to fear. As a matter of fact, I don't think they were brought in, just the riders who were with the herd."

"And what happens to the herd?"

"Your cattle have been rounded up. They're being held down on Spring Creek against whatever fines and damages Judge Thomson will find against you in the morning and I wouldn't gamble on their being light. The judge has lost some fine stock to Texas fever the past year, and he looks with considerable disfavor on anybody who tries to break the quarantine. . . . I had your pa taken down to Bothwell's undertaking parlor. You can go down there and see about making arrangements as soon as you feel up to it tomorrow."

"Thank you," Chuck whispered.

"You've nothing to thank me for," Kincaid said shortly. "I'm sorry for what happened. If I'd been there. . . . Well, there's all kinds of ways of enforcing the law, but some take patience and experience, and Will Reese is young and hotheaded. Maybe I put a little too much responsibility on his shoulders too soon. But you remember this: Will was my deputy when he fired that shot. He was a duly sworn officer of the law, which you men were engaged in breaking. Don't try to make a personal feud of it, understand? I'll have no young Texas firebrands starting gunfights in my jurisdiction. I know what you're thinking—it's plain on your face—but if you kill Will Reese, son, on any excuse whatever, I'll see you hang!" The sheriff turned on his heel and strode to the door and stopped. After a little pause, he looked back over his shoulder. "McAuliffe?"

"Sir?"

"What the hell was your pa trying to do, anyway? Surely he didn't expect to ram a herd of cattle illegally through the sovereign state of Kansas by brute force."

Chuck shook his head. He thought for a moment. It seemed inadvisable to mention the bearded man they'd known as Netherton; if he was around, he'd have made himself a safe position here somehow. These Yankees all hung together, anyway.

Chuck said slowly, "The Old Man only failed at two things in his life, Sheriff. First off, he couldn't manage to win the war for Jeff Davis, even though he lost an arm trying. That hit him hard. And then it began to look like he wasn't even going to get this herd to Sedalia. When a man who's been successful all his life suddenly finds everything going bad that he sets his hand to . . . Well, after a while, I reckon, something kind of snaps inside him." After he'd said it, he saw that it was very nearly the whole truth.

The sheriff frowned. "Did anything snap inside you, son?"

Chuck grinned briefly. "No, sir, but it sure was a pretty sight, those longhorns going up the hill shaking the ground like thunder, and that posse busting apart like a bunch of scared rabbits." He grimaced. "If you'd been pushed around by mobs of farmers like we have, Sheriff, you'd have got pleasure from it, too."

The sheriff stroked his mustache, perhaps to hide a slight, betraying quirk at the corner of his mouth.

He said hastily, "Well, you'd better rest. You'll need a clear head in the morning, if you're going to do the talking for your outfit in court. And you'd better see to it that your men keep their tempers. The way they were carrying on when I was there just now—threatening to take our jail apart—isn't going to do any of you any good."

The door closed behind him. Chuck looked at the painted panels for several seconds, then sank back to the pillow. Suddenly he was aware of a feeling of utter loneliness. One by one they'd been lost to him, his brother Jim, his mother, Dave, and now the Old Man himself. There didn't seem to be much left of what he'd known as a kid, only the ranch, which would soon go for taxes if no money was forthcoming, and a crew of men all considerably older than himself, and a bunch of feisty steers that the Yankees would no doubt find a legal way of taking from him now, after what had happened. . . .

He awoke abruptly, aware that he'd drifted off to sleep again, and that someone had entered the room. He looked up to see a girl standing by the bed.

"Your supper," she said, adding curtly: "I'm Jean Kincaid."

"Why," he said, sitting up, embarrassed by her presence, and very grateful that he'd been left his shirt, even though his trousers, boots, gun, and Bowie knife seemed to have vanished, "why, thank you, ma'am."

Her voice was cool. "Save your thanks, Mr. Mc-Auliffe. It wasn't my idea, you may be sure, turning our house into a rest home for roughnecks who get themselves hurt trying to terrorize decent people!" She set the tray down on a small table beside the bed, and started to turn away; then she swung quickly back to face him. "You had no right to say that!"

Chuck frowned, bewildered. "Say what, ma'am?"

She said breathlessly: "I was in the other room. The door was open; I couldn't help overhearing . . . You've no right to call somebody a murderer just because he has the courage to stand up against a crazy old . . ." She checked herself abruptly.

Chuck looked at her for a moment. She was a tallish girl, he saw, with fine blond hair neatly coiled about her head. She was in the neighborhood of his own age—not much over twenty, at least. Her mouth was too long for beauty, and you might say her nose was, too; and she had a determined jaw to boot. She had long legs, like a colt, and she walked like she was impatient with her ging-ham skirts, and her hands and feet were by no means tiny. Her eyes were blue.

After a moment, she said, "I'm sorry. I didn't really mean—" Her voice trailed away. When he didn't speak, she said quickly: "I really don't think you should go around calling people murderers, Mr. McAuliffe, just for doing their duty!"

"No, ma'am," Chuck said. He took the bowl from the tray, placed it carefully on the blanket between his knees, and began to spoon up the hot soup it contained.

She said, "Of course, we're all sorry it happened, and I can understand how you might feel that . . . Well, it *is* dreadful that Mr. Reese was forced to shoot a man, and I know he's regretting it terribly."

"Yes, ma'am," Chuck said.

The unimpressed tone of his voice seemed to infuriate the girl. She cried, "Ma'am, ma'am, ma'am! Like butter wouldn't melt in your mouth! Stop agreeing with me and tell me what you're really thinking!"

He put his spoon down and looked at her. "Why," he said deliberately, "if you really want to know, ma'am, I'm thinking just what I have right along. I'm thinking your deputy sheriff is a cold-blooded, cowardly, backshooting murderer hiding behind a little tin badge. Of course, you can call me prejudiced, and I can't rightly deny that I am, but you asked for my opinion and there it is."

There was complete silence in the room when he fin-ished speaking. The girl's face had turned pale.

She whispered, "*You* have the effrontery to call an-other man a murderer, Mr. McAuliffe? *You* who come riding into our country with a big pistol on your belt, with your wild cattle, bringing destruction and disease—"

Chuck laughed shortly. "Disease! It makes a handy excuse for turning us ex-rebels away from market, doesn't it? Ask your deputy sheriff just how sickly those cattle looked to him, coming up that hill!"

Her eyes widened with amazement. "You call yourself a cattleman! Are you trying to claim there's no such thing as Texas fever?"

"We call it Spanish fever, or Mexican fever where I come from," Chuck said. "I'd be foolish to claim it doesn't exist. Maybe you've even lost a few head of stock to it now and then, up here in Kansas. But I find it mighty peculiar, ma'am, that every time we get turned back there's some Yankee fellow trying to get our poor ailing cattle away from us, somehow. If they're so damned—excuse me, ma'am—if they're so diseased and worthless, if there's no way of getting them to the railroad, why do these folks want them so bad: the bushwhackers who jump us in the night and try to stampede the herd, the sanctimonious gents who come offering two and three dollars a head, like this Paine who's a friend of your Mr. Reese's? Do you know what I think, ma'am? I have a hunch that once a Yankee gets hold of those steers, you're going to see a miraculous cure. They'll be the healthiest cattle in the state, all of a sudden. And they'll go marching up to Sedalia with the full sanction of the law, to be sold for twenty dollars a head—"

She gasped, "Why, you're quite mad! Do you think my father would stand for anything like that?"

"I wasn't referring to your father, ma'am. He looks like an honest man, for a Yankee. But I can't say the same for his murdering, yellow-bellied deputy."

She said, in a tight little voice she was obviously trying hard to keep quiet and reasonable: "Mr. McAuliffe, I can understand your hatred for . . . for the person who killed your father. It's only natural, I suppose. But you're being terribly unfair. Whatever you may think of our quarantine law, Mr. Reese is sworn to uphold it. What was he supposed to do when you and your father and your hardbitten riders came charging at him yelling like madmen and shooting off guns . . . ?" She drew a ragged breath. "Oh, he's told me all about it!"

Chuck said angrily, "He was entitled to try and stop

us, sure! If he'd stood his ground up there and had his posse fire a volley into us when we came within range, he'd have been within his rights, and I'd have nothing to say against him, no matter who got hurt. We were asking for it, Miss Kincaid, I don't deny it for a minute. But Reese didn't do it like that. When he saw us coming at him, he rode off and left his men to shift for themselves. He took shelter in a draw on the flank. Then I reckon he must have realized there'd be questions asked later by the fellows he'd deserted. He had to make himself look good, somehow, so he waited until we were well past, and came riding out behind us, shooting—" He checked himself, watching the girl's face. He had a sudden, sick understanding that he'd been a blind fool, and a cruel one as well. In the silence, he cleared his throat and asked clumsily: "Is this Will Reese . . . I mean, do you have a special reason for asking about him, ma'am?"

"Yes," she said. Her voice was quite calm now. "Yes, I do have a reason for asking. I'm going to marry Mr. Reese." She walked quickly to the door and looked back. "And I don't believe a thing you've told me!"

He cleared his throat again. "That's fine, ma'am," he said heartily. "Don't you believe a word I've said. All us Texans are terrible liars."

She looked at him for a moment longer. Her blue eyes were wide and dark and wondering. Then she turned and ran quickly out of the room.

13.

AMANDA NETHERTON lifted her skirts discreetly to negotiate the steps leading up to the Kansas Union Hotel, facing the central square of Jepson. Crossing the veranda, she was aware that the loafers comfortably disposed in chairs along its length were watching her, but their glances, while interested, were wholly respectful. This was the frontier, she reminded herself, where women could work themselves to death without protest from anybody, but where they were thoroughly safe from molestation, even from too-bold stares—good women, that is.

Seemingly unconscious of male scrutiny, as custom demanded, she swept through the hotel lobby and down the corridor beyond, head high, eyes modestly downcast. A man coming along the corridor breathed an apology and stood close to the wall to let her pass; she made the briefest murmured acknowledgement of his courtesy. She paused in front of the door to Room 11. The sound of men's voices reached her through the flimsy panels.

She hesitated, suddenly reluctant to enter. Out here she was still the pretty, decorous wife of a traveling cattle-buyer named Bristow. People might discuss, in an idle way, the disparity between their ages; but it was a hard country, and the sight of a forty-year-old man with a twenty-year-old bride was no great novelty: either Bristow had been too busy to get married before, or he'd buried his first wife and maybe even his second. It was nobody's business, and nobody would give it much thought; nor would anyone dream of challenging young Mrs. Bristow's claim to respectability, as long as she dressed and behaved like a lady.

Inside the room, on the other hand, she'd be a common woman consorting with thieves and murderers, receiving no respect from anyone, least of all from herself. Standing there, she made a face, and told herself firmly: *You're warm, honey, you're well-dressed and well-fed, you're even clean—well, as clean as soap and water will make you. There may be a few small spots on your soul that won't scrub out; but what did your soul ever do for you when you were cold and hungry? In any case, it's a little late for you to get finicky now.*

She knocked lightly on the door. The Preacher opened it. She had for him the same contempt she had for all men these days, and it pleased her mildly to see that the side of his face, scraped when he fell from his horse in the general melee south of town—she wished she'd been there to see it—looked even worse now than it had earlier in the afternoon. He'd fashioned a sling for his sprained wrist. It was his gun arm, but with the Preacher that didn't matter greatly. No man dependent on the bottle could be trusted with firearms. He was just a lackey and errand boy, someone with an air of faded gentility who could move about in public without attracting attention or arousing suspicion.

"Thank you kindly, Mr. Paine," she said, curtseying

prettily as he stepped back to admit her. She moved past
him, her skirts whispering, and deposited her armload of
bundles on a chair. Jack Keller was sprawled on the bed
with a glass in his hand, still in the dusty clothes he'd
worn for his ill-fated morning's ride, except for the boots,
which she'd helped him remove. His stockinged foot was
propped on a pillow to ease the ache in his half-healed
leg. "And Mr. Bristow," she said, dropping him a curt-
sey as well. "I hope you took no permanent harm, running from those terrible Texans, Mr. Bristow," she murmured wickedly. "It must have been a harrowing experience. But I forgot, you're accustomed to it; you've
done it before."

She watched his face darken. It wasn't wise to devil
him, she knew, but she couldn't help herself. She had to
keep proving to herself that she still had the courage to
stand up to this man, even though he frightened her—he
was the first man she'd known who had none of the instincts or traditions of a gentleman. Somehow the beard
made it worse. There were just the hard brown eyes and
the big, bony nose—like the beak of a hawk or vulture
—showing through the luxurious growth of curling brown
hair, carefully clipped and groomed now, of course, but
an effective mask nevertheless. What could you do with
a man who never showed you his face? Even his lips
were almost invisible.

"Isn't anybody going to offer a lady a drink?" she
asked quickly, before Keller could speak.

Paine, tall and thin in his black clothes, came forward
to splash some whiskey into a glass for her, taking the
opportunity to replenish his own drink at the same time.
She swallowed deeply, feeling the stuff go down like fire,
and caught a glimpse of herself in the mirror above the
dresser, in her fine blue silk dress, with a small hat on
her smoothly disciplined hair, demure and lady-like
except for the glass in her hand.

She had a moment of wanting to laugh, thinking of the
expressions of the obsequious storekeepers with whom
she'd dealt this afternoon, and of the prim town ladies
with whom she'd passed the time of day, could they see
her now, drinking straight whiskey like a man. She
drained the glass abruptly, and set it aside. There was a
considerable temptation to have another drink, but experience had taught her that one was the right quantity.

It drew a veil over harsh realities, making them bearable, without rendering her stupid or reckless.

"Well," she said, "what have you gentlemen been debating in my absence?"

Keller asked, "What's all that?" gesturing towards the packages.

"Clothes," she said. "The selection wasn't really overwhelming. The local ladies must wear flour-sacks next to the skin."

"Is that a new dress?"

"Yes," she said. "Don't you remember, I ordered it when we first came here? Today, I went for a fitting, and the seamstress had it ready, so I—"

"Haven't you done anything besides buy pretties for yourself?" he asked harshly. "I sent you out to—"

She said angrily, "I know what you sent me for, honey. Was I supposed to go up to the sheriff and ask questions? Did you want me to say: the outlaw Jack Keller and his right-hand man Preacher Paine are at the Kansas Union Hotel and they'd be obliged if you'd tell me—"

"Shut up!" he said. "These walls aren't soundproof."

"I declare, it doesn't seem to bother you when you want to shout!" She drew a long breath, and said quickly: "I talked to the shopkeepers, and to some women who were disposed to be friendly and condescending towards a young bride traveling in a strange country, and to the seamstress. . . . It's all over town. McAuliffe's dead, the old man. The men are in jail. The boy's lying in the sheriff's house with a cracked head." For a woman who prided herself on having dispensed with the luxury of a conscience, she found it strangely difficult to maintain the proper, callous tone of voice. "What else did you want to know?"

Paine was looking at himself in the mirror, touching his scraped cheek with his fingertips. "Did anybody know what those crazy Texans were trying to accomplish with their insane maneuver? Why, they might have killed somebody!"

"That," she said, "is probably just what they were after, friend." She glanced at Keller. "I told you not to show yourself there, remember? The Preacher could have dealt with them alone. I warned you something might happen if they recognized you. I told you—"

"Shut up," he said. "Does anybody know?"

"That you're the man they were after? Nobody seems to."

"That means the hired hands are keeping their mouths shut. What about the boy? Is he fit to talk yet?"

She nodded. "The sheriff seems to've had quite a conversation with him. The way I heard it repeated, he says his daddy just went quietly mad at having his cattle turned back again—I gathered it was the third or fourth time it had happened. The rest, not being very fond of Yankees anyway, just went along for the ride."

"That's all?"

"There was no mention of you, by the name of Netherton or any other. Well, there wouldn't be. I haven't had a lot of experience with Texans, but I know my southerners, honey. It would be a personal matter with them. They wouldn't want the law to have you, even if they trusted the Yankee law to act, which they undoubtedly don't. They'll be hoping to settle with you themselves, some day."

"They're welcome to try," Keller said sourly. "Well, it was your idea to come here. What does the clever Miss Netherton think we should do now?"

She said, "Don't blame me because you went and spoiled everything by showing your face! They came here, didn't they, as I said they would after I'd dropped the name of the town into the boy's ear? If you'd just stayed out of sight and let the Preacher handle it, we'd have had that herd for three or four dollars a head; and with our tame deputy to help us, we'd have been collecting four or five hundred percent profit within a couple of weeks. That was what I advised from the start, remember, when I heard you had the law in your pocket around here—"

The Preacher said quickly, "Not the whole law, by any means. That sheriff is an old prairie wolf; don't underestimate him."

Amanda said, "He could have been decoyed away at the right moment. . . . But you wouldn't listen!" she said angrily to Keller. "You didn't want to put out any money; you were going to get those cattle for nothing; but all you got was a bullet in the leg! I told you times are changing along this border. Some people are going to play it carefully and legally—well, semi-legally, at

least—and get rich; and others are going to stick to their
old violent ways and get hung. I tell you—"

Keller said, "You tell me too damn much, girl!"

There was a little silence, and she saw that she'd gone
too far. It amused him, sometimes, to let her prattle on;
and sometimes he even accepted her advice and used her
ideas; but there was a line and she'd overstepped it.

"Well," she said sulkily, "I want what's best for us,
you know that, and I don't like to see an opportunity
wasted."

He said, "Nothing's wasted, and nothing's spoiled. In
fact, things couldn't have turned out better."

"What do you mean?"

"What's happened to those cattle? You didn't bother
to mention that."

"Why, they've been impounded by the sheriff."

"And what about the boy and the men in jail?"

"They'll go before the judge in the morning. Everyone
expects him to levy a heavy fine, at the very least . . .
Oh," she said. "I see."

"Just so," he said. "We'll get that herd yet, and cheaper
than the Preacher could have bought it off that stubborn old fool." He swung his legs to the floor, pulled
on his boots, rose, and came to her. He looked down
at her critically, and took a fold of the new silk dress
between his fingers. "Very genteel and lady-like," he
said with a sneer in his voice. "I expect the town ladies
were quite impressed. Well, don't let it give you big
ideas, Mandy girl. You aren't running this outfit, and
you're not a lady. Not any more, my dear. You're not
even an officer's mistress. You're just Jack Keller's
woman. Understand?" After a moment, he said, "One
more thing. That deputy. He's losing his nerve. He didn't
bargain for killing, and he's afraid of the sheriff. He wants
to back out. He'll be coming here as soon as it's dark
enough he won't be seen; the Preacher referred him to
me. But I won't be here, and neither will the Preacher.
You will."

She looked up into his bearded face, and read nothing
there, but she realized that she was being punished for
talking too much and too disrespectfully. There were
other ways in which Deputy Sheriff Reese could have
been induced to cooperate, but Keller had chosen this
one deliberately.

"I see," she murmured.

Keller nodded. "You'll persuade our friend to play along with us. How you do it is your business."

"Is it?" she asked. "I thought . . . I thought you said if you ever caught me with another man, you'd kill him and break me in two."

Jack Keller walked to the door, and looked back. He could have been smiling wolfishly. The beard made it hard to tell. "Ah," he said, "but I don't intend to catch you, tonight. Come on, Preacher. . . ."

The door closed behind them. She stood alone in the room and did not move for a long time. Already the light was fading from the windows. She considered refusing the chore that had been assigned her, or doing it badly, and knew she wouldn't. It didn't make that much difference any more. She shivered abruptly, and went to the dresser, and poured herself a small amount of whiskey and drank it down.

Presently she lit the lamp, removed her hat, took off her dress, and replaced it with a frilly, semi-transparent, trailing garment that she'd bought some years back when a colonel in the Union Army had been paying for her clothes. He was the man to whom she'd gone—the first —selecting him deliberately from a number of possibilities, when things had got too bad that winter towards the end of the war, with no food or wood for the fire and the town occupied by Yankee troops. He'd been a man who liked flounces and ruffles; an elderly man who'd treated her like a daughter, except at night. . . .

There was a knock at the door. She gave herself a quick glance in the mirror, patted her hair, and fluffed the pink ruffles at her breasts—they were a little limp and not entirely clean after the miles they'd traveled in her valise across dusty roads, but so much the better. She had made her judgment of Will Reese some time ago. For all his swaggering air, he was a man who might well lose his nerve in the presence of an immaculate and self-possessed lady; but she was sure he'd be quick to take advantage of a semi-intoxicated female in tarnished finery. She poured herself a little more whiskey, just enough for recklessness now, went to the door with the glass in her hand, and pulled it open.

He made a big shape in the doorway. *Well,* she thought wryly, *at least this one's got a face.* As a matter of fact, he wasn't bad to look at, if you liked arrogant young men with big pistols at their hips. She found herself remembering a somewhat smaller youth, also with a pistol but without the arrogance. It wasn't, for some reason, a happy memory, and she put it aside.

"Why, it's Mr. Reese!" she said. "I'm real sorry, Jack's just stepped out. Perhaps you'd care to come in and have a drink while you wait. . . ."

14.

JUDGE THOMSON was a plump, elderly little man with silky white hair, mustache, and sideburns that should have given him an air of gentle benevolence, but couldn't quite overcome the effect of his red, impatient face and sharp blue eyes.

"Five hundred dollars," he said. "Is the defendant prepared to pay the fine now?"

"No, sir," Chuck said.

"You have until tomorrow morning to produce the money," Judge Thomson said. "If you are unable to do so, the sheriff is directed to dispose of the impounded cattle as the law provides, to satisfy the judgment of the court. . . . Mr. McAuliffe."

"Yes, sir."

"In letting you and your men go free, this court is taking cognizance of the personal loss you have suffered. It is hoped that you have learned the lesson that the laws of the State of Kansas are not to be taken lightly. But you are hereby warned that any further acts of violence within our jurisdiction will not be treated with equal lenience. Court is adjourned."

Outside the frame building, that also housed the sheriff's office and jail, Chuck paused in the hot morning sunshine to look around. The two short, wide, dusty streets of the town met here in a small square that boasted a few trees and a new equestrian statue erected to the memory of some Union officer of local renown. There seemed to be a hotel across the way.

There were a number of people in the square, farm-

ers and townspeople both. They regarded the little group
of Texans on the courthouse steps—in their boots and
spurs and big hats—with a kind of wary curiosity, not
actively hostile at the moment, but certainly not friendly.
It occurred to Chuck that he'd felt considerably more at
home the times he'd crossed the border into Mexico, although Mexico was technically a foreign land.

Beside him, Joe Paris drew a long breath. "Well, I've
spent more time in worse jails, but that fresh air smells
pretty good." The middle-aged rider's satisfaction faded
before another thought: "Five hundred dollars! Just because a few mangy steers took it in their heads to run
up a hill! Where the hell does that old buzzard expect
us to scrape up that much cash in less than twenty-four
hours?"

His loud voice drew resentful looks from the nearby
citizens. Chuck said, "Take it easy, *amigo*. Don't work
yourself into a lather. Let's at least get the Old Man
decently buried before we pick another fight around here.
I made the arrangements before coming to court—"

"*Señor Carlos!*"

Chuck looked around quickly. Miguel Apodaca jerked
his head in the direction of two figures coming across
the square. The girl, in a simple, long-sleeved calico
dress, was tall and leggy and had blond hair. The man
was also tall and blond. The silver badge on his shirt
gleamed in the sunshine.

Joe Paris said in a strangled voice, "If I had my gun
back—"

Chuck said, "The man's an officer of the law here. If
we lay a finger on him, we hang."

Joe looked at him, shocked. "Kid, you mean you're
going to do nothing about the fellow who murdered
your dad?"

Chuck glanced at the two approaching figures. Last
night he, too, had been hot with anger—but the anger
had betrayed him into the shameful error of running
down another man, behind his back, to his promised
bride. The truth or falsity of the charges didn't matter;
you just didn't go around telling a girl that her man was
a coward and a murderer, even if he was. The mistake
into which he'd been led by his temper had cooled
Chuck's rage considerably. He'd seen the judgment in

Jean Kincaid's eyes: just another Texas roughneck, careless of whom he hurt with his cattle, his pistol, or his big mouth.

Not that he cared much what a Yankee girl thought of him, but this was clearly no place to be making hasty mistakes of any kind. The vengeful temper of the men, when he joined them in court this morning, had completed the cure. It seemed a little unnatural for him, the youngest of the bunch, to have to play the careful, peaceful role that should have belonged to an older man; but after all, he was the owner now, and somebody had to keep a clear head if they weren't to lose all chance of recovering the herd—not to mention the possibility of rotting in a Yankee jail or swinging at the end of a Yankee rope.

It wasn't as if he was forgiving or forgetting anything, but there were better ways of killing a cat than chasing it around the yard with a dull axe.

He said, watching the big deputy approach, "You didn't listen close to what I said, Joe. I said, he's an officer of the law *here*."

Joe looked at him quickly. "You mean—"

"I mean," Chuck said softly, "somewhere else, like down in Indian Territory, he's just a fellow with a piece of tin on his chest. . . . Come on, the minister's waiting."

He strode off, and the men followed. They all passed within twenty feet of Will Reese and Jean Kincaid, The deputy made some remark to the girl as they went by, and laughed. She didn't laugh, but she looked directly at Chuck McAuliffe and put her hand trustingly on Reese's arm, walking close to the big man, as if to demonstrate that she was giving no weight at all to Chuck's wild accusations of the night before.

The graveyard was slightly up the hill from the little white-painted church at the edge of town. It looked like a small and tidy place for small and tidy people, Chuck found himself thinking, as he listened to the minister's voice declaiming the words of the funeral service with a dramatic fervor that deserved a greater audience than the little group of roughly-clad, bareheaded men standing by the open grave. It seemed like a tame spot for the Old Man to end up, after the places he'd been and the things he'd done.

Chuck became aware of a tightness in his throat and a wetness in his eyes. He turned slightly to hide his weakness from the other men. Then the preacher's words came to an end, and he turned back to help finish the job. He was getting real handy with a shovel, he reflected grimly. The eight hundred miles from Texas had been paid for with human lives. Anybody who thought he'd let those lives go for nothing, just because an old gent with sidewhiskers spoke a few words in a courtroom, just wasn't thinking very straight.

Joe Paris straightened up and blew his nose loudly. "Thirty-five years," he said in a gentle voice. "Since before you was born, kid. We covered a lot of miles together, the Major and me."

"I know, Joe."

They were all around him now, saying one thing and another they thought he'd like to hear; but he wasn't making out the words too well. Always, when someone close to you died, you remembered the things left undone and unsaid, now that it was too late. . . . He swung blindly away and started walking towards the neat, white cemetery gate.

"There's one more thing we have to do for him," Joe Paris said, walking alongside. "How do you figure on getting this deputy down into the Territory, kid?"

Chuck said, "I figure he'll go of his own accord, more or less."

"How's that?"

Chuck glanced at the older man. When he spoke, his voice was bitter: "We've got no more chance of raising that fine than of waving our arms and flying to the moon. We're not supposed to have. These Yankees are all in cahoots, the way I see it. They've got their hands on our cattle, and they're not about to let go in a hurry. If we'd had five hundred dollars among us, the judge would have made it a thousand. I'll bet you the bank's got its order, and anybody else with money in town. No Texan's going to raise a cent in Jepson today, not if he's got solid gold bars for security."

"You could be putting it a mite strongly," Joe said, seeming a little disturbed by Chuck's vehemence. "I

fought the Yankees for four years. It didn't make me
fond of them, by a long shot; but I don't figure they've
all got hoofs, horns, and tails, either; or that their favor-
ite pastime is eating little Texas children. . . . Anyway,
what's this got to do with that murdering deputy?"

Chuck said, "I'll try to raise the money this afternoon, sure. They'll expect me to, and I wouldn't want
to disappoint them. I won't get it. That means the cattle
will be put up for auction. But the fellow who buys
them is going to have to move them out of the state; it
would look a little too raw if they let him ignore the
quarantine completely. And there'll likely be an officer
of the law along to see him across the line, and maybe to
protect him from us wicked Texans. I'm guessing the
officer will be Reese. He seems to be taking a personal
interest in our herd, and the sheriff's not going to waste
time on a little chore like that, not when he's got a
deputy to do the riding for him. And when Reese has
finished the job, he'll likely be coming back towards
Jepson alone." Chuck paused. "It'll be like shooting a
duck on a millpond."

Joe Paris frowned. "Listen, kid—"

Chuck said savagely, "Don't talk fair play to me,
hombre! When we get back home, I'll be as fair as the
next fellow. But Mr. Reese and anybody else up here
who gets in the way is going to get just the break they
gave the Old Man and no more, hear? I'm getting just
a bit weary of burying McAuliffes; I'm going to start
burying me a few Yankees for a change. . . . And after
we've taken care of Mr. Reese, we'll go after the
cattle. If we play along now so these folks think we're
properly scared and there's no harm in us . . . Well, if
somebody jumps the outfit in the middle of the night
down in the Territory somewhere, who's to say it wasn't
a bunch of their own Yankee bushwhackers—particularly
if there's nobody left alive to talk? I'm kind of slow to
learn, *amigo*, but I remember my lessons. If they can
play it that way, so can I!"

He stopped, breathless, having gone somewhat farther
than he'd intended. Grief and anger had carried him
away; but now that he'd said it, he had no intention of
backing away from it.

Joe was looking at him uneasily. "I know how you
feel, boy, but I don't think the Old Man would like—"

"The Old Man's dead with a bullet in his back!" Chuck said harshly. "He wasn't sneaky enough for these Kansas psalm-singers. He rode straight at them. I'm not making the same mistake; and if you don't like it, you can make tracks for home!"

"Easy, kid," Joe Paris said gently. "Take it easy. Don't bite our heads off. We're all with you."

15.

RETURNING TOWARDS town, they were met by Sheriff Kincaid on a wiry little pony obviously of Indian origin. The sheriff sat his mount in the loose, careless, un-picturesque way of the old plainsman, to whom a horse was merely a means of getting from one place to another a little more rapidly and conveniently than by walking. Kincaid might have settled down in this farming community to raise a daughter and enforce the law, Chuck reflected, but he didn't ride like any farmer who ever lived. This was a man who'd once spent some time in the places where the first thing you did each morning was to feel the top of your head to make sure your scalp was still on tight. It was something to remember.

"My condolences, Mr. McAuliffe," the sheriff said, stopping before them. "Please believe that I regret what happened. Not that my regrets will bring him back."

"No," Chuck said.

Kincaid studied him for a moment, and shifted his gray eyes to look at the other men. A faint smile showed on his weathered face. "Nothing more unnatural-looking than a bunch of Texas *vaqueros* on foot," he said with a change of tone. "You can pick up your horses and gear at Dance's Livery, just down the street."

Joe Paris asked, "What about our guns?"

"You'll get them back when you leave these parts for good." The sheriff turned back to Chuck. "I located your wagon and horse herd about six miles south of town," he said, "and let your cook know what had happened. I suggest you send these men to wait for you in camp, Mr. McAuliffe, to avoid further trouble."

"We're making no trouble, Sheriff," Chuck said.

Kincaid shrugged. "Whether you make it or somebody else, it's still trouble, and my job is to prevent it.
Send them out of town, son, so I can quit worrying
about them. . . . Oh, and another thing. There's a
stranger named Paine at the hotel, who says he's got a
contract to supply beef to some Army posts. He was
asking me about your cattle. I thought I'd let you know,
since you'll be trying to raise some money."

Chuck looked up sharply, but the older man's face
seemed innocent of guile. "A stranger?" Chuck said.
"I took him for a local citizen."

"You've met him?"

"Why, yes," Chuck said. "Your deputy brought him
down to us, yesterday. Paine made my dad an offer of
three dollars a head. The Old Man didn't like it. That's
what set off the ruckus."

Kincaid frowned. "Well, I didn't know Will Reese was
acquainted with the fellow; but then Will and I haven't
had much to say to each other since I bawled him out
yesterday." He sighed. "It's made things kind of un-
comfortable around the house, since the boy's going to
marry my daughter and she's already taking his part;
but it's time Will learned that wearing a badge doesn't
entitle him to be quite so free with his fists and gun. . . .
Ah, well, I don't suppose any father ever found a young
man good enough for his only female child." He paused,
and looked at Chuck narrowly. "You wouldn't be trying to hint there's something crooked between Will Reese
and this cattle-buyer, would you, McAuliffe? Just because he brought the man down to talk to your dad?"

It was obvious that Jean Kincaid hadn't repeated to
her father much, if anything, of what she'd been told last
night. Chuck hesitated. The sheriff saved him the trouble of finding an answer.

"If you are," Kincaid said coldly, "you might as well
go right ahead and call me a crook, too, young fellow.
Because I'm advising you right now, if you haven't the
money to pay your fine, to go see Mr. Paine. I hate to
say it, three dollars isn't much, but it's more than you're
likely to get if I have to auction off that herd of yours
in the morning. Nobody around here's likely to pay more
than hide money for wild Spanish cattle that can't legally
be brought to market. I suggest you go talk to this Paine
and see what kind of a proposition he'll make you. Even

if his price is plain robbery, maybe you can sell off a couple of hundred head for enough to pay the judgment against you. Better than losing the whole herd."

"All right," Chuck said. "I'll talk to him."

"And get these men out of town. I don't want them hanging around getting drunk and quarrelsome."

"Yes, sir," Chuck said meekly. "I'll see that they leave just as soon as they've got their horses."

The sheriff regarded him a moment longer, clearly unconvinced by this show of tractability. He seemed about to make some further comment, but decided against it and rode away. Chuck watched him go, thoughtfully. Kincaid appeared to be an honest man. On the other hand, it was kind of odd, when you came to think of it, that every lawman in the region should be so dead set on having Mr. Paine get the cattle he wanted at the price he wanted to pay. . . .

16.

BACK HOME, Jean Kincaid drew the living room curtains against the hot morning sun. Her father did not seem to have returned from the courthouse, where she'd seen him last; at least he didn't answer her call. She stood in the semi-dusk of the room, pulling off her bonnet and gloves, aware of Will Reese closing the front door and coming towards her. She turned to face him, smiling.

"Well," she said, "that's that!"

He didn't understand what she meant, of course; and he frowned slightly. Then, as she'd hoped he would, he took her in his arms and kissed her instead of asking questions. As always, his kiss was rough and demanding; but then, older women had warned her not to expect much consideration from any man, in this respect. It seemed to be generally agreed that men were all selfish and thoughtless where their pleasures were concerned; and Will, she had to admit, was certainly no exception to the rule. It was clear that her life as Mrs. Reese was going to be no sweet and romantic idyl such as one read about in the books considered suitable for young ladies.

766 **TEXAS FEVER**

Well, she'd never taken much stock in those silly stories, anyway, having been raised in a country where a story-book young lady who swooned in times of crisis wouldn't be looked upon with much favor. As a girl, she'd seen her mother die with a Pawnee arrow in her back—had held her on the wagon seat, as a matter of fact, since her father had been too busy urging on the wildly running team. She'd seen too many weak and kindly men broken by the hardships of the frontier, leaving their families destitute, to be cared for by neighbors.

Life was one thing and book romances were another. Will Reese might not be much of a hand at gentle courting, but he was a good man and he would, she'd been assured by the ladies who'd taken it upon themselves to advise a motherless girl, make a fine husband and provider—and if she didn't snap him up, there were other girls in town both ready and willing.

Anyway, she wasn't made of glass, and there wasn't any sense acting as if she'd break, even though she might have preferred a relationship based upon a little more ... well, respect and dignity.

"Will!" she said sharply. She freed herself, and turned away to rearrange the bodice of her dress. "That . . . isn't decent," she said.

He was silent for a moment. She thought he was angry; then he laughed and came up behind her to put his big hands on her shoulders.

"What's decent?" he murmured. "We're to be married, aren't we?"

"Well, wait until we are."

"Waiting's hard on a man," he said, a little sulkily. Then he laughed again, and turned her around to face him. "You're pretty when you're mad, honey."

"I'm not mad," she said, smiling. After a moment, she said, teasingly: "As pretty as that little Mrs. Bristow staying at the hotel?"

Even as she said it, she'd have given a great deal to recall the words. She hadn't intended to bring up the subject at all, but somehow it had slipped out—and in a way she was glad. It was hard enough, two people learning to live together, without making it worse with deceits and concealments, even well-meant and harmless ones.

She felt his hands leave her shoulders. When he spoke,

his voice sounded puzzled. "Mrs. Bristow?"

She looked up at him sharply. "Will," she said, "you're not going to claim you never met the lady! Why, it's all over town, and Bess Donohue, who was helping her father at the hotel desk last night, came over this morning to make quite sure I wouldn't put any misinterpretation on your visit in the room. Wasn't that kind and thoughtful of her? The little Irish alley-cat!"

"Oh," he said. "*Bristow*. . . . I'd forgotten the name of Paine's partner. Why, his wife seemed like a very charming lady, but a little high-toned for mere country folks like us. I found it hard to make conversation with her, waiting." He laughed abruptly, looking down at her. "So *that's* why you've been parading me around town this morning, honey!"

She flushed slightly. "Well, I didn't want anyone to think I believed their nasty stories. Will," she said, "who's Mr. Paine?"

He shrugged his broad shoulders. "Just a man with whom I've done some business in the past."

"And Mr. Bristow?"

"I told you, he's Paine's partner. They're cattle-buyers. They . . . wanted to know the procedure, if these Texas cattle should be auctioned off; I think they might be interested in putting in a bid. I wasn't quite sure about it myself, so I asked at the courthouse, and went over to tell them what I'd learned, afterwards, but they were out. Mrs. Bristow said they'd be right back. I waited a while —as a matter of fact, you can tell Bess Donohue I had a drink of whiskey; that should scandalize her properly —but they didn't return, so I left. Is there anything else you'd like to know?" His voice had a sulky note again.

She said quickly: "I didn't mean to sound as if I was cross-examining. . . . Will," she said, "was it wise?"

"To have a drink with Mrs. Bristow?" He laughed. "Of course not. The way people in this town seem to stick their noses in everybody's business, I should have taken to my heels the minute I realized the lady was alone!"

"I wasn't referring to that," she said. "But I see no reason for you to run errands for stray cattle-buyers. Can't they get their own information at the courthouse?"

He said, rather irritably, "I told you, Paine's an old acquaintance. I saw no harm in doing him a favor."

"I just mean—" She gestured towards the badge on

his chest. "The law isn't supposed to do people favors, my dear. Somebody might get the impression—"

His voice was suddenly harsh. "What impression?"

"Well," she said, "these Texans, for instance, already seem to have the idea that we wicked Yankees lie awake nights dreaming up new ways to victimize them. The young man who was here—of course, he was half-crazy with grief, not to mention the crack on the head—but he made all kinds of ridiculous and fantastic charges—"

"Charges?" Will demanded. "What charges?"

His tone was loud and unpleasant; and she had a sudden feeling that the scene was slipping out of control in a frightening way. What should have been merely something for them to laugh about tolerantly—the town's proclivity for constructing outrageous gossip out of any material, no matter how flimsy—seemed to have led them into grim and desperate matters threatening their whole future together. The big man before her reached out and grasped her shoulders again, almost shaking her.

"What charges?" he cried.

"Will!" she protested, trying to free herself from his painful grip. "Please!"

He did shake her now. His face was ugly with rage. "Are you going to take the word of strangers and jealous females like Bess Donohue against mine?"

"But, my dear," she said, agnast, "I wasn't . . ."

Then she stopped, looking up at him in horror, seeing him clearly for the first time: a weak man, guilty and afraid. It came to her suddenly that everything that had been charged against him was probably true—and if it wasn't, it could be. This was a man who could deliberately shoot another man in the back, whether he'd actually done so or not. This was a man who couldn't be trusted with any pretty woman, if she gave him encouragement. Whether Mrs. Bristow had been complaisant or virtuous didn't really matter; what mattered was that she could have had him if she'd wanted him. Any woman could have. . . .

"Let me go, Will," she said quietly.

For a moment, she thought he was going to strike her. Then his hands dropped. "All right!" he cried. "All right, if you're going to believe. . . !"

He didn't finish the sentence, but turned and stormed

out of the house, slamming the door behind him hard enough to rattle the pictures on the wall. After a little, she brought her hands up to rub the bruises his big hands had left on both shoulders. She stood like that, hugging herself as if cold, for a long time.

17.

CHUCK MCAULIFFE watched the crew ride out of town reluctantly. After they'd gone out of sight, he swung about and started walking towards the square. Little boys looked after him wide-eyed, impressed by his big hat, Bowie knife, and high-heeled boots, but the adult glances he received were cold and unfavorable, reminding him that he was alone in enemy territory. The war might be over, but it wasn't forgotten, whatever Sheriff Kincaid might claim.

At the hotel, he arranged for a room, since he could hardly impose on the sheriff and his daughter for another night. Asking a question, he was told that Mr. Paine had room number nine, down the hall to the right. Chuck hesitated, shrugged, and went down the indicated corridor—not that he expected to accomplish much of value there, but it would not hurt for him to be seen docilely following the sheriff's advice.

Knocking on the door with the proper number, he received only silence for an answer. He rapped a second time, waited, and was about to turn and depart when the door of the adjoining room opened, and the thin, soberly clad figure of the cattle-buyer appeared, swaying. Obviously, his garments were all that was sober about Mr. Paine, at the moment.

"What the hell do you . . . Oh." Paine frowned with an effort of concentration. "It's young Mr. McAuliffe, is it not? My deepest sympathy in the matter of your bereavement, friend. In the midst of life, as the saying goes . . . What do you want?"

"I'd like to discuss some business with you, Mr. Paine."

Paine steadied himself against the doorjamb. "Friend,"

he said thickly, "I am, as you can certainly see, in no condition to discuss business, and in no mood, either. Now, if you had pleasure on your mind, Pythagoras Paine would be your man. . . ." His voice grew suddenly sharp. "Come back in the morning. I'm busy. Good day."

He started to retreat into the room, with dignity, and was about to shut the door in Chuck's face, when a male voice from behind him said, "Let the young man come in."

It was a voice that sounded familiar to Chuck, although he could not recall where he'd heard it. Mr. Paine looked startled. He turned his head. "But—"

"I said, let him in!"

Paine shrugged his shoulders helplessly and expansively, flung the door wide, and stumbled to one side. Chuck stepped forward, and stopped short inside the doorway. Facing him from the big chair was a tall, bearded figure that he might not have recognized even though the right leg was propped up on a low stool as if lame or injured —but there was no doubt of the identity of the smaller person who sat on the arm of the chair, with the man's hand at her waist.

Chuck was aware of the clink of bottle against glass, to one side, as Mr. Paine helped himself to a fresh drink, but for a moment he had eyes only for the girl. She was very different in appearance from the smudged and trailworn young lady he'd once kissed beside a campfire, at her own request. He could not imagine himself venturing to touch this stylish, silk-clad lady, although he could not help noting that the man he'd known as Netherton —though Chuck had seen him only once, in the dim interior of a wagon, it could be no other—seemed to have no similar qualms.

The position of the man's hand, and its small, possessive, explorative movement along hip and thigh, was a familiarity no decent woman would have endured, certainly not in public. It made the relationship between them very clear, as well as the morality of the girl permitting the caress—not, Chuck reflected, that he needed any more evidence on this point, after her behavior that night. Honesty forced him to recall, however, that his own actions hadn't precisely followed the rules of strict propriety, either. . . .

He found the girl watching him with, he thought, a hint

of amusement. He felt his ears become warm; and he turned his attention hastily to her companion.

"Close the door, Mr. McAuliffe," the man said.

Chuck reached behind him to close it. He was past the first shock of recognition now; he was remembering clearly who this man was and what he'd done, and he let his hand, returning, come to rest on the hilt of the knife at his belt. The seated man smiled—at least his lips changed contours among the shrouding whiskers—and moved the hand that was not engaged with Amanda Netherton. The blanket on his lap slid aside, to display a large revolving pistol aimed directly at Chuck.

"Let's not be hasty, boy," he said.

Chuck looked at the weapon, with a coolness that surprised him. "Fine words," he murmured, "for a man who breaks camp hastily in the middle of the night."

The bearded man smiled more widely. "It seemed indicated. Mandy, here—" His hand slid upwards and came to rest cupped affectionately about a breast discreetly indicated by the close-fitting blue silk of the girl's bodice. "Mandy, here, thought we might have visitors. Her instincts—in such matters, at least—are usually correct."

"We did come looking for you, at that," Chuck admitted.

"With what purpose in mind, boy?"

"Why," Chuck said, "We were going to hang you."

There was a little silence in the room; then the bearded man threw back his head and laughed heartily. "Hear, Mandy? They were going to hang us!"

Chuck found himself as acutely aware of what the man held in his caressing left hand as of what he held in his threatening right. He saw the girl, annoyed if not actually embarrassed by this public fondling, make a move as if to rise, but the man's big fingers clamped down hard, causing her to wince with sudden pain. After that, she sat quite still.

Perhaps, Chuck thought, he was supposed to come charging to her aid, but it was hardly the occasion for misplaced chivalry. He might not be able to help blushing like a fool, but he could damn well keep from getting killed like a fool—although it did seem like no proper way to treat a woman, whoever and whatever she might be.

"Not both of you," he said. "Dad said we don't make

war on females, so we just brought one rope."

"And the crime for which I was going to hang?" the man asked. "What was it?"

"Murder," Chuck said.

"I don't call it murder when two men shoot it out face to face. Your brother had as good a chance as I did; he just didn't shoot as straight."

Chuck looked down at the predatory, half-concealed features of the man in the chair. "You're not denying it, then?"

"Hell, no. Why should I?"

"The law calls it murder, I reckon," Chuck said, "when the man who's killed is engaged in defending his property, and the man who kills him is engaged in stealing it."

"Ah," said the bearded man, "but now you're straying from the subject. What the law says isn't of much importance between us, is it, boy? That is, unless you're planning on turning me in to the local sheriff." He laughed. "I hear you and your pa didn't have much luck setting the law at Baxter Springs on our trail. Almost wound up in jail yourselves, didn't you? I shouldn't think you'd care to repeat the experiment, but you're welcome to try."

Chuck said, "I had the notion Sheriff Kincaid was pretty honest, according to his lights."

"Sure. According to his lights. He might even arrest me. But I'd come up before a Yankee judge and a Yankee jury—and I should think you Texans had had enough of Yankee courtrooms for a while. By the time they got through with the trial, boy, you wouldn't know which of us was up for murder, you or I."

"That may be," Chuck said dryly, "but if you shoot me with that pistol there won't be any doubt of it."

The man chuckled, and lowered the weapon. "Just a precaution, in case you turned out to be a hothead. I'm glad to see you're a reasonable young fellow, instead." He sat up abruptly, releasing Amanda and pushing her off the arm of the chair. She would have fallen if she hadn't managed to catch the foot of the nearby bed to steady herself. To this, the man paid no attention, watching Chuck closely. "What brought you here, anyway?"

Chuck said, "The sheriff told me Mr. Paine had been making inquiries about the cattle. He thought maybe I could sell off a couple of hundred head for enough to pay my fine."

Keller looked at him for a moment, and chuckled. The chuckle grew into a laugh that had the bearded man gasping for breath. Abruptly, he stopped laughing and composed his face.

"The Preacher's not buying anything tonight, as you can see," he said, with a gesture towards the bed. The black-clad man had sat down upon it to finish his drink; now he was lying sprawled across it, inert, the empty glass still in his hand. In his black clothes, he had the look, Chuck thought, of a raven, dead and partially decayed. The man in the chair leaned forward. "You young fool!" he said. "Why should we buy a couple of hundred of your steers tonight when we can get the whole damn herd at auction in the morning? Now, you listen to me, boy, and listen close. . . ."

He paused to shift his leg on the stool, wincing. Chuck said, "I'm listening."

The bearded man looked up. "My name's Jack Keller," he said harshly. "You may not have heard of me down in Texas, but folks through Kansas and Missouri know me. Some call me an outlaw, but they're mistaken: there's never been enough evidence for a warrant to be issued against me, and I've still got friends in high places. They'd damn well better stay friendly, too. There was a lot of raiding and fighting through these parts, before the war and during it. It was done in the name of slavery or abolition—take your pick—but the motives weren't always as pure as they were claimed to be; and a lot of respectable citizens performed acts they wouldn't care to be reminded of now. They'd shake in their boots at the thought of Jack Keller on the witness stand, on trial for his life; they'd pull any string they could to prevent it. So don't count on seeing me legally hanged for murder. You'll just make more trouble for yourself if you try to accomplish that."

Chuck said, "We'd already come to that conclusion, the night you left us. That's why we brought our own rope."

Keller frowned. "If you've still got revenge in your mind, don't be a fool. I've killed more men than you've got years; and if you try to plant that young machete in my back, you'll be dead before you ever get within

striking or throwing distance. As for your cattle, you've
already lost them, so why not resign yourself to it? The
loss is a small one, since you weren't about to sell them,
anyway—not with the local people feeling the way they
do. So take my advice, boy, just gather up your crew
and head back to Texas. Chalk it up to experience. Even
a jackass has more sense than to keep butting his head
against a stone wall. Now get out of here!"

Chuck hesitated. Jack Keller's hand lifted the pistol
again, not threateningly, but warningly. The girl was still
standing by the foot of the bed. It occurred to Chuck
that she hadn't spoken a word since he entered the room.
Beyond her, the drunken man on the bed breathed noisily
through his wide-open mouth. Chuck looked down at the
big pistol, and turned deliberately, and walked away
from it without haste, the way the Old Man had ridden
away from those guns at Baxter Springs. At the door,
he looked back.

"There's just one thing, Mr. Keller," he said.

"What's that?"

Chuck cleared his throat, feeling a little self-conscious
about what he had to say. "You don't have to worry
about your back, sir. Should I decide not to take your
advice, you'll see me coming."

18.

AMANDA NETHERTON waited until the door had shut
behind the compact figure of the departing Texan; then
she whirled angrily to face Jack Keller, but something
in his manner made her withhold the sharp words she'd
been about to utter. He was grinning at her in a way that
made her uneasy. He rose from the chair, tested his bad
leg gingerly before trusting his weight to it, and came
to stand over her.

She said, but not as strongly as she'd intended, "You
didn't have to maul—"

"Sure, I did," he said. "Now the boy knows whose
property you are, if he didn't before. . . . Come on, let's
get the Preacher to his own room." He turned and limped
around the end of the bed. "You take the feet," he said,

and frowned when she did not move. "Well?"

Anger betrayed her into being unreasonable. "Carry your own drunken companions!"

He looked at her for a moment, his eyes narrow. "Take the feet, honey," he said softly.

She hesitated, but instinct warned her not to make an issue of it, and she approached reluctantly. Together, they half-carried and half-dragged the slack figure of Preacher Paine into the adjoining room and dumped him on the bed there. The unconscious man moaned slightly, and his lips moved.

"Gather around, friends," he muttered, "gather around while I expound on . . . on the virtues of Professor Pythagoras Paine's Perfected Pills. . . . Step up, friends . . . are you suffering from . . . suffering. . . ." His voice trailed off into an incoherent mumble. Then he said with sudden clarity: "The game was quite honest, gentlemen. You have no grounds for complaint. Go home and learn to play cards. I warn you, if you come any closer, I will shoot to kill!"

Jack Keller chuckled, looking down at him. "Damned if he didn't do it, too! Dropped two of those fine welshing gentlemen dead in their tracks with the pair of der-ringers he wore up his sleeves. It was a fool thing to do, but after a while, I guess, a man gets tired of being stepped on and pushed around by the nice folks who make all the rules and interpret them to their own bene-fit. I saved his neck from a rope that night. He's been with me ever since. . . . Help me get his boots off, the poor sot."

There was a kind of impatient sympathy in his voice that made her wonder if she had misjudged him; she hadn't thought him capable of an emotion as soft as sympathy. Strangely, it made him seem more, rather than less, formidable. She assisted him without protest; but after they'd gone back to their room, pride forced her to return to the attack.

"You didn't have to humiliate me in front of that boy."

He turned the key in the lock, and straightened up to look at her. "You're Jack Keller's woman," he said. "I wanted him to know it, and not be carrying any romantic notions about with him. There's nothing as unpredictable as a kid with a head full of romantic ideas. Besides, you've been putting on a few too many airs, lately. . . .

It's funny how, the minute you give a woman a handsome dress, she's got to try to live up to it." He grimaced. "Well, that's all right for the townspeople, Mandy, but don't you put on any airs with me."

"Airs!" she said hotly. "What . . . what I did for you last night, I suppose that was putting on airs!"

He laughed. "I don't think you found it too unpleasant, honey. Our deputy is a fine-looking man; you've known worse, I'm sure. You might even be able to do something profitable with him, if there was anything inside him. But there isn't, which is why I have no worries about your trying to use him against me. You're smart enough to know there's no future in a man like that. Now, this young Texas lad, that's another matter entirely. He's got some growing up to do, but you'll note he didn't feel any need to prove how brave he was, looking into the muzzle of a gun. He didn't rant or bluster or threaten how he was going to cut me into little pieces and feed me to the coyotes. . . . He's considering a plan of his own, I think. I wish I knew what it was."

She said, "I could find out for you."

"You could find out," he said dryly. "But I'd never be quite sure it was for me, would I, Mandy?"

She said, "If you question someone's loyalty long enough, my dear, something's apt to happen to it."

"Loyalty?" he said, and laughed. "Honey, I'm not an old fool of an army colonel, or a young fool of a lieutenant, either, or any of those others you wound around your fingers with your haughty tricks, all the while laughing at them because you weren't giving them anything that really mattered. Were you? It was just a game you were playing without committing yourself, letting them have the use of your body occasionally in return for certain practical considerations. . . ." He didn't continue with the thought, but stood looking down at her appraisingly. "I knew a woman like you once, Mandy," he said. "It was . . . well, never mind where it was. She was taller than you, and her hair was black, and her name had a Frenchy sound, and she ran a place on the river, but she had the same way of holding her head high and looking at men as if they were dirt."

"I don't—"

"Oh, yes, you do; my kind of men, at least." He laughed again. "When we met, you weren't in any posi-

tion to be proud, if you'll recall. You'd just made a big,
expensive gesture, throwing everything he'd ever given
you back into that fool lieutenant's face. You were shabby
and broke and hungry, but you were still doing me a
favor by just deigning to speak to me, like a princess
in exile. That's what I nóticed, honey, that look. A
princess condescending to mingle with commoners—mingle is a pleasant word for it!—while she awaits the sum-
mons to return to her kingdom. The first time a man
sees that look, there's nothing he won't do to help. The
second time, he's wiser. It's the second time for me,
Mandy."

"I see," she said, since she had to say something.
Never before had he spoken of his past, though he'd
made a point of inquiring into hers, and she wasn't sure
she liked him in this reminiscent and analytical mood
—not that she was overly fond of him in any mood.
"What happened," she asked, "with the Creole girl? I suppose she was Creole."

Keller laughed grimly. "Why, she took me for three
thousand dollars and a diamond ring, honey. It wasn't
hard. I was young; I thought I was tough and clever, but
I was like biscuit dough in her hands. Hell, she had me
reading books to improve myself. I was going to quit
what I was doing, never mind what it was, and become
a good citizen, and take her away from that evil place.
... I didn't even have a gun or a knife on me, the day she
laughed in my face and had me knocked on the head and
thrown out—I guess, when I saw what a fool I'd been,
I tried to kill her with my bare hands. It was never very
clear in my mind, afterwards. When I was able to return,
the place was closed and she was gone. I never did find
her. I expect she'd made her pile; she probably went
east with it, representing herself as a wealthy young
heiress or widow woman. She's probably got a big house
now, and a respectable husband in a stiff collar and
hard hat, who doesn't know she's laughing at him every
day of his life. That was what she wanted, respectability.
She'd lost it somewhere along the way; and she was
fighting to get it back. Just like you, Mandy."

She threw a glance around the hotel room, with its
stained wallpaper and rumpled bed. "If respectability's
what I want, I'm surely looking for it in strange places."

He said, "You don't fool Jack Keller. You came with

me only because you smelled quick money; and if you ever get your hands on enough of it, you'll leave me— leave me dead, if necessary."

She said indignantly, "I've just proved that, haven't I? If I'd wanted you dead, I could have left you down in Indian Territory, raving in delirium."

He smiled through his beard. "Ah, but I haven't made you the money yet—or stolen it for you—the money that's going to buy your way back to your kingdom, your place in society. . . . You'll never get it from me, Mandy. I think you're beginning to catch onto the fact that you've bitten off more than you can chew. There isn't a woman smart enough or tough enough to take Jack Keller a second time. That's why you're looking around for another way, like this young Texan, with his big ranch way down where nobody ever heard of the South Carolina Nethertons and the poor unfortunate daughter whose name is not to be spoken, the one who sold herself to Yankee officers instead of starving honorably like a lady should—"

She hit him then. Her own violent reaction took her by surprise. She hadn't realized how deeply his sly voice had cut and probed, searching out the weaknesses in the defense she'd built around herself. . . . A princess in exile, indeed! She felt the harshness of his bearded jaw against her palm, and took pleasure from the rough contact. An instant later she was on the floor, and the whole side of her face was oddly numb except for a burning, stinging sensation. Half-dazed, she didn't quite understand what had happened; then she heard his voice:

"You women! Use your hand on a man and expect him not to strike back? Get up!"

She put her hand to her bruised cheek, incredulously. It was the one thing that hadn't happened to her; despite the life she'd led since the war, she'd never before encountered deliberate physical brutality—a man who got a little rough when he was drunk wasn't the same thing at all. Usually he'd be shamed and apologetic and very generous in the morning. But there was no hint of regret or apology in Jack Keller's face; and she realized that the capacity for violence was what she'd sensed in this man, what she'd feared, and now that she'd made the error of calling it forth, she had no idea of how to cope with it.

He took a step forward. She saw, aghast, that he was

about to kick her, and she scrambled to her feet without dignity, aware that her hair was coming down and her clothing was awry, and that some hope or illusion to which she'd clung for years was broken inside her.

"That's better," he said harshly. "When Jack Keller says jump, you jump." He looked at her with a kind of possessive contempt, and flicked his fingers, backhand, across her face. "Princess," he said.

19.

At the bank, Chuck McAuliffe met laughter again. The banker, a portly man with a heavy gold chain decorating the expanse of his fine waistcoat, thought it a great joke that a boy hardly old enough to shave should be asking his respectable and conservative institution to hazard its money on a bunch of scrawny, disease-bearing longhorns.

"Five hundred dollars?" he asked, chortling. "Young man, I admire your gall, but I wouldn't give you five cents for all the wild cattle in Texas, and neither, I assure you would anybody else in this town in their right mind. Personally, I doubt very much that there'll ever be a real market for those misshapen animals. Might as well ask me for a loan on a herd of buffalo."

"Thank you, sir," Chuck said politely, having expected no other answer. He'd come here for the same reason he'd approached Mr. Paine: if he seemed to be doing his best to retain his cattle by legal means, people would be less likely to suspect him of planning something violent and illegal. Whoever bought the herd in the morning, whether Paine, Keller, or someone else, there was no sense in putting that person on guard.

Thinking thus, Chuck came out of the bank into blinding sunshine, and, preoccupied and momentarily dazzled, ran squarely into the tall figure of Will Reese. The collision threw Chuck back against the wall.

He heard Reese swear. "Why don't you watch where you're . . . Oh, it's you! I've been looking for you, McAuliffe!"

Chuck straightened up. "Reckon you've found me."

The bigger man's face was grim. "I hear you've been lying about me, kid, telling folks I shot your dad from behind."

Chuck looked up quickly. Reese's voice had been unnecessarily loud, pitched to carry across the street. Already, sensing trouble, several townsmen were drifting closer to watch, while a woman coming down the walk turned and sought shelter in a nearby store.

Chuck said, "I figure the location of the bullet-hole speaks for itself, Mr. Reese."

"I can't help it if the man turned just as I fired."

"If he'd known you were there," Chuck said deliberately, "I can promise you the man wouldn't have turned *away* from you, sir!"

"No? He saw me coming and started to flee, that's how it happened."

Chuck said, "The Old Man never ran from a Yankee in uniform. Seems unlikely one with a badge would scare him." He drew a long breath. "If it's a fight you want, Mr. Reese, just give me a gun and let's get at it."

The blond man laughed. "Mighty cocky all of a sudden, aren't you, kid? You didn't look so brave yesterday when I rode you down. You can be thankful I'm a merciful man. I had every right to shoot you, too, for resisting arrest."

Chuck said dryly, "Seems I recall seeing you scratching around mighty hard trying to find a pistol. . . . In any case, I'll save my thanks for that wall-eyed plug you were riding. And you can be grateful I was there to stop him or he'd still be running." He breathed deeply again. "If you haven't a gun to spare for me, sir, our Bowie knives'll do fine—or don't you care for cold steel up here in Kansas?"

At the back of his mind was the sheriff's warning: *You kill Will Reese, son, on any excuse whatever, and I'll see you hang!* But it was too late to think of that now. There had been no choice, anyway. Obviously Reese had looked him up for the express purpose of picking a fight; and he wasn't going to avoid it. There were times to be careful, but this wasn't one of them, with the Old Man's murderer standing there asking for trouble. The consequences would just have to look out for themselves.

He heard Reese laugh and address himself to the growing crowd: "Listen to the bloodthirsty little rebel

wildcat!" The big deputy was unbuckling his gunbelt.
"Kid, you're in civilized country now. We don't settle our
quarrels with bloodshed here. What I'm going to do is
just give you a good thrashing."

Chuck stared at the big man, shocked. Where he'd been
raised, the idea of settling a dispute barehanded never
occurred to any male old enough to wear long trousers.
Only kids and animals fought with the implements pro-
vided by nature: pummeling somebody with your fists
was barbaric and undignified and unheard-of among
gentlemen. If you were a man, you used a man's weapons:
the knife or the gun. If you hated strongly enough to fight
at all, you hated strongly enough to kill.

Reese had passed his gunbelt to one of the spectators.
Now he unpinned the badge from his shirt and dropped
it into his pocket.

He winked at the spectators. "A little private business," he said. He turned to Chuck, and his handsome
features settled into heavy, cruel lines. "I'll teach you
to tell lies about me behind my back!"

A cold sensation of fear went through Chuck McAuliffe
as he watched the larger man approach. He'd faced death
several times along the trail, and he could face it again;
but the idea of being smashed and beaten before an eager
audience seemed more frightening than being killed. Then
a wry sense of humor came to his rescue, and he
thought: *Looks like you've gone and talked yourself into
one hell of a licking, my friend. Now you just go and
take your medicine like a little man!*

With the thought, he put his head down and charged
directly at Will Reese. The sudden onslaught caught the
deputy by surprise. Chuck's head took him squarely in
the stomach, and both men went off the sidewalk and
down into the dust of the street together. Chuck found
his feet and started flailing at the larger man's head as
Reese, breathless, struggled to get up.

For a moment, the advantage was Chuck's, and he
did the best he could with it, but Reese quickly got his
arms up, shielding his face as he rose. Chuck switched
his attack to the body and got in two hard blows; then a
big fist came from nowhere and knocked him sprawling.

Groggy, he sat up and saw the tall deputy coming towards him. Reese passed a sleeve across his mouth to
wipe away a trickle of blood. His eyes were narrow and

bright with cruel anticipation. Chuck rolled aside, avoiding a kick, and rose. Instinct told him that, as the smaller and quicker man, he'd do well to stay clear of his adversary; but there was no real doubt in his mind of the outcome of this, and if he was going to get licked he might as well get it over. Dancing around out of range wouldn't accomplish anything except maybe give him time to lose his nerve.

He moved in fast, therefore, ducked inside Reese's whistling swing, and started pounding with all his strength at the taller man's midsection. A short, hard blow to the side of the head sent him staggering aside; and a carefully aimed fist knocked him down. He rolled over, scrambled up, and bored in again blindly, head down. There were only two directions to go, and as long as you were moving forward you might not be accomplishing much but at least you weren't running away.

He was knocked down again. He got up dazedly, found the big shape of his adversary against the sun, and moved in grimly, swinging. His arms were getting tired now and his nose was bleeding. He took a couple of glancing blows and, winded, managed to get in close enough to throw his arms about the larger man, pinning Reese's arms to his sides, but the deputy broke free and swung a fist, low, that drove the last remnants of breath from Chuck's body. As he doubled up, Reese clubbed him over the head. He went down in the dust and knew that he would now be kicked into unconsciousness by the other's boots, but he was incapable of making a move to save himself. . . .

Nothing happened. After a little, he heard a voice that he recognized as belonging to Sheriff Kincaid. It sounded angry. Reese answered. He sounded angry, too. Hands picked Chuck up and set him on his feet and supported him there. He blinked and saw the sheriff standing before him.

"You all right, son?" Kincaid asked.

Chuck felt a cut inside his mouth with his tongue. He spat into the dust at Kincaid's feet. They were all Yankees and he hated them all.

"Sure," he said thickly. "I feel real fine. You got any other deputies in need of exercise, sir?"

Somebody laughed. Kincaid's face remained sober. "Take him over to the hotel," the sheriff said to the men on either side of Chuck. "He's got a room there. Take care of him."

There was kind of a gap after that. Presently he was in his hotel room, on the bed, and somebody was pulling off his boots, while somebody else cleaned the blood from his face with a damp cloth, not very gently. He looked up at the two strangers working over him.

The one at his feet said, "You've got the nerve and the speed, kid, all you need is somebody to show you how to handle yourself, and you could give even Will Reese a pretty good battle."

He looked at the two of them, hating them. He said, "We don't fight like dogs down in Texas," and turned his face to the wall. But after they'd gone, he started feeling badly about it. After all, they'd tried to be kind, even if they were Yankees. . . .

20.

CHUCK CAME awake abruptly, without knowing what had aroused him. It was dark in the room, except for the dull rectangle of the window and the streaks of slightly more intense light defining the outlines of the ill-fitting door. Then the latch rattled, and one of those streaks widened to admit the weak yellow illumination of the lamp above the stairs at the end of the corridor.

It took Chuck a moment to recall the appearance of the room by daylight, and the disposition of his few belongings—in particular the fact that he was lying on top of the bed, fully dressed except for his boots. He could feel the Bowie knife bruising the small of his back, on the right side, as he lay there; and he turned his body cautiously to make the weapon available without causing the springs of the bed to creak. He found the hilt with his hand. Then, very slowly, watching the door, he began to draw up his knees to give himself leverage for a sudden move.

The door was still opening slowly. He could see part of a figure there, black against the light, holding something in one hand. It was unmoving for the moment, apparently listening for signs of wakefulness on the part of the occupant of the room. Suddenly the door swung wide, and light struck the bed directly. Chuck snatched out his knife and rolled to the floor, got his feet under him, and hurled himself towards the door—might as well be shot going that way as trying to jump out the window, the only other exit, two stories off the ground.

There was no explosion, no flash of gunfire, no shock of a bullet to check him; and at the last moment, ready to drive home the heavy, partially two-edged blade, he realized that the figure awaiting him had the bell-shaped silhouette of a woman rather than the clothespin-shaped silhouette of a man. He heard a woman's gasp of fright, and his hand brushed the silk of a woman's dress. Then, as he recoiled, he heard a woman's soft laughter.

"Carefully, Mr. McAuliffe, or you'll cause me to drop the bottle, which would be a shame." After a moment, she murmured, "If you're quite finished with the acrobatics, please cover the window before you make a light."

He stood for a moment, foolishly, panting from his effort, suddenly aware of the bruises and contusions that he had not had time to consider sooner. He shrugged his shoulders briefly, sheathed the knife, and went to the window, aware of her entering and closing the door behind her. In the ensuing darkness, he made his way to the lamp.

When he turned—the room fully lighted now—she was still standing just inside the door, dressed as he had seen her last. She made a pretty, fashionable picture in the dismal hotel room, except for the whiskey bottle in her hand and the great bruise that disfigured one side of her face.

She saw his eyes widen. "Don't stare, Chuck," she said. "You look a trifle battered yourself, come to that." Her skirts rustled as she turned towards the dresser, where stood a glass and a pitcher of water. "Only one glass?" she said.

He licked his lips, puzzled and embarrassed by her presence. "What do you want, ma'am?"

She said without turning her head, "Why, misery loves company, I reckon. I heard you'd had some trouble. I thought we could have a real interesting evening together, talking about what it feels like to be beaten. . . ." Her voice died away. She poured some whiskey into the single glass, turned, and came across the room to him, her clothes whispering. "You'll have to drink out of the bottle, my dear," she said. "It's a knack I haven't learned yet, although the way I seem to be heading, I'll probably master it soon."

There was bitterness and self-contempt in her voice. She held out the bottle, and he took it mechanically. She raised her glass to him. "What do you say down in Texas?"

He said, "I believe the Mexicans say *salud,* ma'am, but to be honest, I've had little experience with hard liquor. . . ."

"Well, it's time you learned," she said. "You're a nice boy, Chuck, but you'd better start growing up fast, if you expect to get back those cattle of yours."

He frowned. "How do you know I—" He checked himself, quickly, flushing.

She laughed. "Like I say," she murmured, "you're a boy. It's obvious to anybody that you have some terribly wicked plan in mind. Jack Keller would like to know what it is."

He asked, "Is that what you're here for, ma'am, to find out for him?"

She shook her head. "I don't care what your plan is, Chuck. I don't want to know what it is. I just want to be sure it succeeds." Her fingers touched her hurt cheek delicately. "Jack Keller's got his eye on that herd, too. There are other herds, but you-all hurt his pride down at the Arkansas, you shook the confidence of his men in his leadership, and he's got it fixed in his mind now that he's going to get those particular cattle before any others. And Jack Keller eats nice little boys for breakfast without bothering to spit out the bones." She raised her glass again. "*Salud,* Charles McAuliffe."

He hesitated. It was perfectly clear in his mind that the bottle could be drugged or poisoned, or, more probably, that she'd come here for the express purpose of getting him drunk and talkative. He certainly had no cause to trust her. She was, he reminded himself, the person who had decoyed them to this town where the Old Man had been killed; she was obviously Jack Keller's mistress; and what she'd said about wanting his, Chuck's, plan to succeed didn't seem very plausible, on the face of it.

On the other hand, the marks of Will Reese's fists

were still plain and painful on his body, and it wasn't pleasant to remember that he'd been licked, even if by a bigger man. And the girl before him had made matters no better by talking to him as if he were a kid: he was in no mood for caution. Anyway, he'd never learn her motives in coming here unless he played along.

He'd had no experience with serious drinking, but he had, of course, tasted the stuff on the sly as boys will; he remembered enough about it not to take too much at once. He didn't cough or choke on it, therefore, but moisture did come to his eyes. . . . He saw that Amanda Netherton was lowering her glass, empty, and smiling at him.

"It's perfectly good liquor, you see," she murmured.

He flushed slightly. "I didn't think it wasn't."

"There's no need to be polite. Of course you thought so; you'd have been a fool not to. You're wondering why I'm here."

"I will not," he said, "question my good fortune."

Her laugh rang out, delighted and happy as he remembered hearing it once before. She clapped her hand over her mouth, aghast; and they stood listening for a moment, but the hotel was silent about them. She laughed again, softly.

"Why, that was a real polished and grown-up speech, Mr. McAuliffe."

He said, rather stiffly, "Now you're making fun of me, ma'am."

Her laughter died. "I don't mean to," she said. "I swear I don't mean to." After a moment, she reached up and touched his cut lip with her fingertip. "Did he hurt you badly?"

Chuck grimaced. "He damn near . . . excuse me, ma'am, he almost knocked my fool head off, but I reckon I asked for it."

"Asked for it?" she demanded, frowning. "How?"

"A man ought to be careful what he says, even when it's the truth. I talked myself into that licking."

She made a little face, and felt of her cheek tenderly. "You're very philosophical about it, Chuck. I reckon I talked myself into this, but I declare I can't . . . can't resign myself to being knocked around like . . ." She stopped, and looked down at her empty glass, and held it out. "One more, I think," she said. "That should be about right."

He started to ask her meaning, but thought better of it. He poured whiskey into her glass, to the level she indicated, wishing suddenly that his brother Dave was handy to advise him. Dave would have known what to make of this girl who drank hard liquor like a man, who let herself be fondled and beaten by an *hombre* like Keller, and who still managed to retain a certain air of quality, a look of lost innocence.

He watched her take her drink to the bed, and sit down, and sip deliberately from the glass. She looked up at him, and patted the space beside her. The last thing in the world he wanted to do was sit on a bed close to her —or was it? He didn't know. He did remember very clearly, however, that he'd panicked from this girl once. He hadn't hoped he'd ever have the chance to redeem himself, but he wasn't going to pass it up if it offered itself.

He made himself walk over, therefore, and sit down. He said, "*Salud*, ma'am."

"*Salud*, Chuck."

They drank, and he felt nothing for a moment; then the effects of the whiskey spread warmly through his body. He looked at the small girl beside him and grinned.

"Anyway," he said, "it beats getting licked by Will Reese." He held out the bottle. "Put it away, ma'am. I reckon I've had about enough for a nice little boy."

She smiled and rose, carried the bottle to the dresser, corked it, and set it down. She finished her drink, and set the glass down beside the bottle. She turned to look at him.

"You see," she said, "I'm not trying to get you drunk, as you thought."

"My thoughts seem to be uncommonly easy to read, ma'am."

"Oh, they are," she said, smiling. "You're thinking now that you don't know why I'm here, but you aren't going to be tricked into trusting me one little bit. And still you're remembering that time by the campfire—"

"It's not something I'm likely to forget," he admitted readily, when she paused.

She smiled at him across the room. "Would you like to kiss me again, Chuck?"

"I reckon I would," he said evenly. "But—"

Her eyes narrowed slightly. "But what?"

"But I'd have trouble keeping my mind on it, ma'am, since I'd be waiting for Mr. Bristow, as he calls himself here, to come busting through that door with a gun and catch me making improper advances to his wife, as you call yourself here. . . ."

There was a silence. Her face had gone a little pale, and tightness had come to her lips; then her features relaxed and she smiled at him approvingly.

"Good boy," she murmured. "You've got all the possibilities figured out, as you should. Mr. Bristow-Keller has hired a rig and left town to make certain arrangements. He won't be back until morning, but I don't expect you to take my word for that. Suppose I wedge a chair under the door knob, since there seems to be no key; would that reassure you?"

He said, "I reckon it would serve."

His voice, he was pleased to hear, was steady enough, although he wasn't quite sure how he'd managed to keep it that way. He watched her prop the chair against the door and come across the room with that soft, feminine whisper of clothing: the lamplight, dull elsewhere, seemed to be shining very brightly in her hair. He knew that he no longer cared why she'd come; yet he wanted her respect, he didn't want to act like a fool boy who could be twisted around the finger of any pretty woman. He waited until she'd sat down beside him again; then he reached out and turned her face and touched the ugly bruise gently.

"You want me to kill him for you?" he said. "For that? Is that it, ma'am? Is that why you're here?"

She said calmly, "You'll kill him, probably. You'll most likely have to, not because of me, not because he killed your brother, but because you both want the same thing, and he isn't a man who'll give up until he's dead. But I didn't come here to ask it of you, although I won't deny I'd like to see it. You'll do it or not, as the situation demands. I just came here to make sure that, if the time comes, you'll stand a chance. No boy is going to beat Jack Keller. I figure it's about time you stopped being a boy, Chuck McAuliffe."

He looked at her, and heard his own voice speaking with that unnatural steadiness for which he had no explanation: "It's easy to say."

She said gently, "It's not hard to do, my dear. Most

boys seem to manage. Now I want you to kiss me, and then you can help me undress. . . . No, we'll leave the light. I'm not modest, and there's no reason for you to be. It's not something one should be modest about, anyway. It's the one thing that's never respectable, no matter how much people try to make it so. . . . Chuck."

"Yes, ma'am," he said.

"Amanda," she said.

"Amanda," he said.

She put her arms about his neck, regarding him thoughtfully. "When you do this, my dear," she said, "when you do this, it's always nice to tell the woman you love her, even if you don't mean it."

He tried to speak, but now the words would not come. She smiled and drew his head down. Her lips were warm and responsive as he'd remembered them, her body was warm and pliant through the layers of clothing, her hands held him close, and the whiskey helped: tonight there was no feeling of shame or guilt, or even any great sense of urgency. When they overbalanced, in each other's arms, and fell to the bed together, the springs let out a great groan; and suddenly they were lying there, looking at each other in the lamplight and laughing. She sat up, presently, and pulled the pins from her hair, and shook it loose. It fell about her shoulders, shining redly, the way he'd first seen it.

"Amanda," he said, watching her.

"Yes."

"I love you," he said.

"Yes," she said. "Now help me off with my dress, there's a good boy. . . ."

21.

AFTERWARDS, lying in bed beside her, he was aware of a feeling of release and revelation, and he knew that nothing would ever be quite the same again. He could look back tolerantly, as if over miles of distance and years of time, at the young kid who'd come up the trail, cocksure and ignorant, brash and scared. He felt strong and adult and confident, and he kissed her lips lightly,

and allowed his hand to trace the shape of her breast,
firm and smooth to his touch. It seemed quite natural to
take this liberty, until she stiffened slightly against him.
He took his hand away.

"My apologies," he said, a little hurt.

She laughed softly, and took his hand and replaced it
where it had been. "Don't be silly. You just . . . He bruised
me there, this afternoon."

"Do you want me to kill him?" He asked it quite
calmly.

"No," she said. "I don't *want* you to kill anybody. I
don't think it's a pleasant thing to have to live with.
But if the necessity should arise, I don't want you to have
any childish scruples, either. Killing a man is like taking
a woman, Chuck. Those who fail at it are those who
think too much about it. It's something that, when the
time comes it should be done, you just go ahead and do."

He murmured, "Have you killed so many, then,
Amanda, that you can speak of it with authority?"

She laughed. "No, but I've known men who have,
army officers and . . . and others." He knew a little
pang of jealousy at the thought of the other men she'd
known; apparently she sensed it, because she went on
quickly: "Sometimes they'd talk about it. Don't forget.
If the time comes, don't think about it, or worry whether
it's right or wrong. He won't be thinking or worrying,
you can be sure. Just do it. Like . . . like you did this,
tonight."

It seemed, at first glance, as if there was little con-
nection between the two things, one dealing in life and
the other in death; yet when he reflected upon it, he
realized that, somehow, she was right. They were both
facets of the same mystery, a little of which had been
revealed to him tonight.

He said abruptly, "The nearest town is called Sabrina."

Her eyes opened to regard him widely. "Nearest to
where, my dear?"

"You could wait in town," he said, "but the hotel is
a poor place. You'd better go straight out to the ranch.
It's close to fifty miles, but Henry Espenshade, at the
livery stable, will have somebody drive you out. I'll give
you a note to Pablo Aguilar, who's looking after things
at home. Like I told you, the house isn't in real good

shape, but you'll be comfortable enough. With any luck,
I should join you before very long."

"And then?" she whispered, still watching his face with
that curious, intent look.

"Why," he said, "then we'll be married." She did not
speak, and after a little he went on: "I'd like to take
you with me now, but the trail's no place for a woman—
as you've learned—and there may be trouble along the
way. It's better that you go down the river and come into
Texas from the east. I'll have to figure where to get you
enough money for your fare—"

She said, "Chuck McAuliffe, you're a fool!"

He looked at her in mild surprise. She sat up, heedless
of her nakedness, and stared down at him angrily. He
thought he'd never seen anything near as lovely as she
looked, sitting there, with her long hair loose about her
bare shoulders. There was a funny, tight expression
about her mouth and eyes, as if she were hard put to
keep from crying.

He said calmly, "I see nothing foolish in what I said."

She said breathlessly: "Just because we . . . You don't
have to marry me, you idiot! You don't want to marry
me!"

"As for having to," he said, "I don't know about that.
As for wanting to, I reckon I'm a better judge than you
are."

She cried, "You're no judge of anything! You're just
a boy who's taken a woman to bed and figures he's made
a great discovery. Well, maybe you have, but I assure
you it's a discovery you can make with any woman, any
time. It's got very little to do with marriage, with two
people living together day after day, year after year.
You're not going to spend the rest of your life in bed,
my dear!"

He grinned, lying there, and said lazily: "At the moment, I could think of worse—"

She went on without heeding him: "You're going to
spend your life among other people, in that little town
you just mentioned, Sabrina, and what are you going to
tell them when they ask about your new bride? A man
wants to be proud of the woman he marries! Are you
going to tell them the truth? Are you going to tell
them you married a little trollop you took away from

an outlaw named Jack Keller because he was mistreating
her and you felt sorry for her?"

He reached up and began to wind a lock of the long
chestnut hair about his finger. "No need to be so hard on
yourself, Amanda."

She slapped his hand away. "Hard? I know what
they'll say, all those good people! Hard? There's nothing
like your fine, righteous citizens for hard!"

"They don't need to know," he said. "Not that I care
if they do. The McAuliffes have run Clear Creek without
advice from Sabrina; I reckon they can get married
without consulting Sabrina. And I reckon the folks of
Sabrina will be civil to Mrs. McAuliffe, whoever she
may be, or we'll just pull their town down and build us
a new one with better manners."

Her mouth trembled, and composed itself firmly against
this weakness. "You see!" she said. "Already you've
wiped out a town full of people because of me!"

He chuckled. "It was a pleasure, ma'am. You want
San Antone or Austin razed to the ground, just say the
word."

She stared at him blindly for a moment, and began to
cry, the tears running down her cheeks unheeded. He sat
up and reached out to touch her, but instead he got up
and extinguished the flame of the lamp, throwing the
room into darkness. Then he got back into bed and
drew her down beside him, still crying, and covered them
both with the sleazy blanket.

"You don't understand," she gasped. "You . . . you
just don't understand what kind of a person . . . You don't
know what I've been!" She went on quickly, before he
could speak: "Oh, I know what you're thinking! You're
thinking I'm a tragic victim of fate whom you're going to
save from a life of shame. Well, I've always managed to
keep some such notion, myself, until today. I've told myself that somehow I'm finer and better than the girls
who . . . who work in . . . I've seen myself as a clever, cal-
culating adventuress; a brave, free soul. . . . Brave! I'm
a coward, Chuck. When he hit me, this afternoon, there
was nothing left but . . . but jelly. I'd have said anything,
done anything, to make him stop. And I realized suddenly that I've always been a coward, running from the
slightest pain or discomfort, running anywhere, to anybody who'd promise to take care of me. . . ."

He said, "You seemed to be bearing up real well under pain and discomfort when we met on the trail."

"But you're wrong!" she whispered. "I was trapped into that. I couldn't refuse to go along and help when I heard he was hurt. I owed him that much; besides I needed him, or thought I did. . . . I had brave plans for using him. And all the time he knew what I had in mind and was laughing, waiting for the right moment to . . ." She stopped, and put her hand to her bruised cheek. Chuck did not speak, and after a moment she went on: "And I didn't bear up at all out there; I turned to you, don't you remember?"

"I remember," he said, "But—"

"Oh, it was deliberate and cold-blooded, my dear," she said. "It should tell you what I am. After a week or so I'd had enough of nursing a sick man, of being tired and frightened and dirty. I was looking for someone who'd take me away from . . . Keller knows me, he's a devil for reaching into a woman's soul and holding up to scorn all the trashy little illusions with which she tries to deceive herself. He showed me the truth about myself, this afternoon." She drew a long, ragged breath. "And if I should let you marry me, and there should be hard times on your ranch, I'd doubtless run off with the first well-dressed traveling man who promised a fine meal and a new dress!"

He said placidly, "I'd come after you, and shoot the fellow, and bring you back."

She was silent for a little; then she whispered, "Now you've razed a town and killed a man. Because of me. Can't you see? I'll bring you nothing but trouble, my dear!"

It was a capitulation, and he kissed her gently. "We'll sleep now," he said. "In the morning, early, before Keller gets back, I'll take you down to camp. You'll be safe there until we can arrange how you're to travel."

22.

AMANDA NETHERTON stirred in the darkness, disengaging herself cautiously from the arms of the boy beside her. Then she waited a little, but his breathing remained steady and undisturbed. She slipped out of bed and stood looking down at him for a moment—not that she could see more than the vague shape of him, sleeping there, but she could imagine the way he looked: an odd mixture of boyishness and sunburned toughness. He was a real sweet boy, and she should have known how he'd react to being . . . well, seduced was the proper word for it, no sense mincing matters. Perhaps she had known.

The thought frightened her. She'd thought of it as a valiant gesture, a way of showing herself that she still had the courage to defy Jack Keller, even though the thought of his big fist now made her sick with fear. There was also the fact that she liked this young Texan and wanted to help him: an experienced woman could do much for a youth at this point in his life. He needed confidence if he was going up against Jack Keller. She could give it to him. It was a way of paying her debts to both of them.

She'd been going to do this, and slip out into the darkness afterwards—she'd determined where she could hire a rig, even at this hour, and her belongings were packed and ready—she was going to disappear before the Preacher awoke from his drunken stupor, or Keller returned. She was going to leave this place, these people, this life, and start afresh somewhere. . . .

Now she shivered abruptly, knowing that she was not by any means brave enough to carry out this plan: she'd never really intended to. Deep down inside her, without admitting it, she'd known that, after making love to her, Chuck McAuliffe would not let her go. She'd known that, being young and chivalrous, he'd feel obliged to ask her to marry him; and she'd known, too, that she would let him persuade her to agree.

And in the morning, not too far away now, he'd wake up and look at her, not with the eyes of a boy intoxicated

104

with his first discovery of manhood, but with the eyes of a man. He'd know he had been tricked, but he would stand by his word, being a nice boy. He'd take her to his camp, and Jack Keller would come for her there, and men would be killed, maybe Chuck McAuliffe among them. And if not there, then down in Texas. His crew knew what she was; it was no secret. Sooner or later, back home, one of them would speak, and sooner or later some man would pass a remark in Chuck McAuliffe's honor, and he'd feel obliged to buckle on his big pistol in defense of his wife's honor.

And, sooner or later, as this went on, she'd probably become the rich young widow McAuliffe, without much reputation, perhaps, but with a house and lands and cattle, and maybe she'd planned that, too. There seemed to be no end to her cleverness.

She shivered again, and began to dress hastily in the darkness. Finished, she started for the door, but paused to pick up the whiskey bottle: if it was gone in the morning, Jack Keller might be suspicious. A little missing liquor would be no cause for comment, however. He'd just assume she'd drunk herself to sleep. The thought would please him. She knew now that he meant to destroy her, deliberately, slowly, savoring each step in her downfall, and she would let him. After today, she'd be afraid to fight back.

The chair made a clatter as she pulled it away from the knob. The boy on the bed gave a deep sigh and moved; he seemed to be reaching for something, or someone. Then he was quiet again.

She stood there a moment longer. It had been a beautiful dream: a husband, a home, a place where nobody knew. . . . But there was no such place. There was only this dingy hotel, and she'd better get back to her room before people started moving about and saw her slipping down the stairs with her hair down and her clothes half unfastened and a bottle in her fist. After all, here she was still, publicly, the proper young Mrs. Bristow—although certain glances she'd received yesterday seemed to indicate that even this false respectability had become somewhat tarnished since Will Reese's visit of the night before. Either he'd been seen or he was a man who liked to boast of his conquests, maybe both.

The packed valise stared at her accusingly when she

reached the sanctuary of her room—hers, at least, until
Keller returned. She walked past it to the window and
looked out at the dark, endless prairie, wondering how
she'd managed to deceive herself that she'd ever dare
venture out there alone, even with a road to guide her.
She'd had quite enough of that, driving aimlessly through
the rain with Jack Keller delirious in the wagon behind
her. If they hadn't run into the McAuliffe herd, they'd
both be dead out there now.

To be sure, she'd thought fast enough—and talked
fast enough—after help was at hand; you had to give
her credit for that. Nobody could deny she was clever.
But all her cleverness couldn't get around the fact that
she was trapped in this dusty frontier town until Jack
Keller chose to take her elsewhere—she certainly couldn't
depart by stage without his knowing it. *No woman runs
out on Jack Keller,* he'd said.

She wheeled abruptly, turned up the lamp, and walked
across the room to the dresser. Her face looked back at
her from the spotted mirror, disfigured by Keller's blow.
Only a boy in a poorly lighted room could have found
her attractive, she reflected grimly, as she picked up a
brush and began to brush her hair. The bruise would heal,
but there would be other blows, now that the man had
discovered the efficacy of the treatment. He'd probably
beat her half to death if he learned what she'd done tonight, as he was bound to. Because Chuck McAuliffe,
finding her gone, would come looking for her. Tricked or
not, he'd feel obliged to, even though secretly he might
regret his hasty offer of marriage.

The boy would come here to claim her, openly, unarmed except for his silly great knife, and Keller would
shoot him down. . . . Her brush-strokes faltered and
stopped. Suddenly she buried her face in her hands and
began to cry helplessly. It was a trap she'd led them both
into, assuming a courage she did not possess. There was
no escape.

23.

Awakening, Chuck McAuliffe was immediately aware that he was alone, but he wasn't at first quite clear in his mind why this should be a cause for concern. After all, he'd awakened alone in his bed or blankets every other morning of his life.

Then the events of the night came back to him, and he opened his eyes and sat up quickly. The room was quite empty. There was no sign of his midnight visitor. He might have dreamed the whole incident; except that he knew he had not. It had happened, there was no doubt about that.

He got up and dressed quickly, wondering why she had slipped away. He also found himself wondering, in the cold light of morning, just what it would be like to be married. Well, that card was played. There was no picking it up now, even if he'd wanted to. It was just a matter of finding her and talking sense into her again, if necessary; and if anybody had any comments about his choice of a bride, they could damn well refrain from making them aloud. A McAuliffe paid his debts and kept his word.

He clapped his hat on his head and went down the stairs, aware again of the bruises and lacerations picked up in his fight with Will Reese. It seemed like a long time ago . . . if you could call it a fight, he reflected ruefully; it had been more of a massacre, the way he remembered it. Well, that was another debt that would be paid before long. At the foot of the stairs, he paused to regard the people in the lobby and the high sunshine in the square, visible through the door beyond. He must have slept like a bear holed up for the winter.

The lateness of the hour made him uneasy; and although he'd had some thought of taking a circumspect look around first, he turned and walked down the corridor directly to Room 11, and knocked on the door. Waiting, he reached back and felt the hilt of his knife: if Keller was inside, and wanted trouble, trouble was what he'd get.

107

He heard a sound of movement and stepped back, but
the man who opened the door was not Keller, or Bristow,
or whatever he chose to call himself. It was Mr. Paine, the
one they'd called the Preacher, in his rumpled black
clothes, with bloodshot eyes. He opened the door only a
crack, and peered out warily.

"Who is it?" He frowned at Chuck. "Oh, it's you
again, friend. What do you want now?"

It did not seem wise to announce his mission, and
Chuck said, "Why, you said for me to come back in
the morning. I thought you might have reconsidered. . . ."
Something about the man's furtive look aroused his sus-
picion, and he asked, "What are you hiding in there?
Is anything wrong?"

"Wrong?" The Preacher's voice was smooth. "What
would be wrong, friend? As for reconsidering, I believe
my . . . my associate gave you your answer last night,
and I see no reason to misdoubt his judgment."

"Where is Keller? Maybe I could persuade him—"

Paine said, "Mr. Bristow sent a message that he'd meet
us at the auction down on Spring Creek. I'd say he expects to buy some cattle there; and it seems highly unlikely that you can persuade him to give you money to
defeat his purpose. Now, if you'll excuse me . . ."

He started to withdraw, never having opened the door
more than six inches. Chuck moved abruptly, putting
his boot into the crack as it started to close.

"Just a minute, friend!"

There was a brief scuffle. The older man tried to kick
away the obstructing foot. The Bowie knife gleamed in
the opening, and Paine recoiled, letting the door swing
free. Chuck pushed it wide, and stepped inside cautiously,
knife ready, watching the man before him but ready for
attack from either flank. With his elbow, he swung the
door fully back against the wall, assuring himself that no
one was hiding behind it. He stepped clear of it. There
seemed to be no one in the room to explain the Preacher's
wary attitude. Then Chuck became aware of the still
figure in the bed.

The Preacher spoke. "I suggest that you close the door,
my boy. . . . That's better."

Chuck stared at the motionless shape of the girl.
She was lying there with her hair outspread on the pillow

and her lips slightly parted. Her eyes were wide open, looking at nothing.

Chuck whispered, "What . . . who . . . ?"

"Turn the key in the lock . . . so." The older man's voice was soft. "Now I think you can sheath that menacing weapon, young man. I did not kill her, I assure you." After a moment, watching him, the Preacher murmured: "I see. You came here to find her, is that it? That would seem to indicate that she visited you last night, before. . . . What happened? Was your virtue unassailable, friend? Did she find in you no shining knight to come to her rescue? Is that why she . . . ?"

Chuck turned his head. "Be quiet, old man."

"Yes," Paine said. "Yes, to be sure."

Chuck stared at him for a moment without seeing him clearly. Then Chuck turned, shoving the big knife back into its sheath, and walked slowly up to the bed. He hesitated, and reached out and closed the staring eyes, as he'd seen it done more than once along the trail. He noted that there was a small bottle of medicinal appearance on the coverlet near her hand.

"Laudanum," the Preacher said, behind him. "It's very popular for the purpose. There would have been no pain."

Chuck said dully, "I asked her to marry me. She was going to Texas to wait for me."

"I see." The older man's voice was gentler. "My apologies, then. To both of you."

Chuck swung to face him. "What do you mean?" Paine did not speak, and Chuck demanded: "What are you doing in here?"

The Preacher shrugged. "After the messenger from . . . er . . . Mr. Bristow awakened me, I found myself requiring a little stimulant. There was none in my room so I came in here. She was lying as you see her. Then you knocked on the door. . . . I suggest you take your leave now. I will do what's necessary. I was . . . quite fond of her, myself. In a fatherly way, of course."

Chuck said quickly, "I've no intention of leaving her—"

"Of course you're leaving," the older man said. "You can do nothing for her now, nothing that I cannot do as well. What can you accomplish by staying, except make trouble for everybody?"

"But—"

"You young fool," the Preacher said, "if she did it foɪ anyone, she did it for you. Think about that. Will you spoil her last fine gesture for some notion of pride? Now get out of here . . . Oh, pass me that bottle on your way. Thank you."

Chuck paused at the door. "What will you do?"

"Why," Paine said dryly, "I'll discover her, of course, and give the alarm, in a state of shock and distress. As soon as I've built up my strength to a sufficient degree." He shook the bottle in his hand, and measured the level of the liquid with his eye. "First I will contemplate the fact that small oblivion can be found in large bottles, and large oblivion in small ones. There must be a philosophical truth involved, somewhere. Good day, sir. . . ."

24.

WALKING ALONG the square, Chuck was barely aware of the warmth of the sun on his head and · shoulders. *If she did it for anyone,* Paine had said, *she did it for you* . . . . He remembered, with shame, his rueful thoughts about marriage upon awakening. Perhaps she had known he would feel like this in the morning. Perhaps she had killed herself, rather than hold him to his promise. In any case, he felt like a coward for having left her with no one but an old drunk to look after her.

Thinking like this, he was only vaguely aware of an open buggy driving up beside him.

"Mr. McAuliffe."

He stopped and turned. Jean Kincaid was looking down at him from the buggy seat. She was wearing the same calico dress he'd seen before, and her fair hair was softly arranged under her neat bonnet.

"Is . . . something amiss, Mr. McAuliffe? You look so—"

"No," he said curtly, "nothing's amiss, ma'am."

"And if it were," she said wryly, "it would be none of my business, would it?" After a moment, she went on: "I thought you'd be down at Spring Creek for the auction. Dad rode down early."

He'd taken off his hat politely enough, but he couldn't manage to put any politeness into his voice. He said, "I think the coyotes can fight over the carcass without me watching."

She smiled at this. "Dad being one of the coyotes, Mr. McAuliffe? You don't like us very much, do you?"

He said, avoiding a direct answer, "I'll be leaving town as soon as I can, ma'am. I'm just waiting around to get our guns back—assuming nobody figures out a nice legal way to separate us from those, too. I reckon there's folks around here who'd just love to send us back through Indian Territory unarmed; and it would surely bring happiness into the lives of some of those Cherokee braves we scared off on the way up."

She was still smiling. "You certainly do have a high opinion of us! But you shouldn't be in too much of a hurry to ride off. You'll have some money coming to you from the sale of the cattle."

Something about her pretty air of tolerance was more than he could stomach. In her demure dress, holding the reins firmly in her small gloved hands, she seemed to represent everything he hated about this northern country—also, the mere fact that she was alive seemed to be a direct insult, under the circumstances. She was alive, well fed, neatly dressed, and smugly proud of herself for all the advantages she had that were none of her doing. She'd never known what it was to be part of a defeated nation; she'd never known misery and shame; the thought of taking her own life, under any circumstances, would never have crossed her mind. . . .

He knew that he should keep quiet; but suddenly he had to tell someone exactly what he thought and felt. At least he could wipe that infuriating look of smiling forbearance from her face.

He shook his head. "Money?" he said, "No, ma'am, I'm not really counting on any money."

"What do you mean?" she asked quickly.

"Why," he said deliberately, "I figure it's already been arranged for the herd to go for the exact amount of the fine and costs. Your dad warned me not to expect much, and the fellow at the bank was kind enough to tell me nobody around here has much interest in Texas cattle. That seems to leave it up to these here visiting cattle-buyers Paine and Bristow—if you want to call them that

—and I don't reckon anybody's going to embarrass a fine, upstanding Yankee citizen like Mr. Bristow by making him pay any more than just what's necessary to make the transaction look all legal and proper."

Her smile had faded. She said, shocked: "You don't really believe—" She checked herself. "I can understand your resentment, but you're being terribly prejudiced and unfair!"

"Unfair!" he said explosively. "What's fair about us driving a herd of cattle eight hundred miles, at the cost of three lives from our own crew not to mention a few other deaths along the way—there was a little hard work and suffering involved, too, ma'am—only to have them taken away from us by a bunch of fine sanctimonious gentlemen who never slept on the ground or saw a river in flood!"

She said, "Mr. McAuliffe—"

He went on hotly: "You want me to ride down there and watch them throwing dice to decide who's going to get my cattle for how much? No, thank you, ma'am! I'm staying right here in town and being a real good boy. That way, maybe I'll get out of this nest of Yankee thieves with what's left of my shirt. If I went down there, I might make the mistake of expressing my true feelings, and get myself thrown in jail for life!"

He had reached her at last. She started to speak angrily, stopped, and jerked her head sharply, indicating the seat beside her. "Come here, Mr. McAuliffe!" she snapped. "Come up here, where I can talk to you properly!"

"Thank you, ma'am, but—"

She said tightly, "You get up on this seat, or I'll take the whip to you!" She reached over to snatch the implement from its socket.

Her anger pleased him. At least he'd managed to penetrate her armor of sweet female hypocrisy. He laughed scornfully and said, "Why, ma'am, did your gentleman friend, the deputy, send you here to finish the job he started yesterday? With a buggy whip?"

She stared at him for a moment, speechless; then she made an odd little sound in her throat, and let the whip drop back into place. She looked almost as if she were about to cry.

"I . . . I'm sorry," she said almost inaudibly. "I don't

know what . . . got into me! You're such a wrong-headed and irritating person. I . . . I lost my temper. Please. Come up here so we can talk. You can't really believe all those things you said. . . . We can't keep shouting at each other like this right here in the middle of town, there'll be no end to the scandal. . . . Please?"

He hesitated, but she'd made her apology, and he could do no less than comply with her request, without seeming stubborn and ungracious.

"Very well, ma'am," he said, and climbed in beside her.

She shook the reins and spoke to the old bay gelding between the shafts. Neither of them said anything for several minutes after the rig was in motion. Then she spoke without looking at him.

"I suppose I'm responsible for . . . for your trouble yesterday, Mr. McAuliffe. I shouldn't have . . . I didn't mean to repeat what you . . . But Will knew I'd talked to you, and when I let slip . . . He was terribly angry."

Chuck said dryly, "Yes'm, I noticed that."

"Did he hurt you very much?"

Chuck moved his shoulders. "I reckon I've taken worse lickings. Your dad stopped it before he got a chance to use his boots."

She winced. "If it's any satisfaction to you, I'm no longer engaged to marry Will Reese."

He looked at her quickly, startled. "I'm sorry, Miss Kincaid. I never intended—"

"I'm sure you didn't." Her voice was tart. "You just go around making all kinds of reckless accusations, and it never occurs to you that . . . that someone may be . . . hurt." She bit her lip. "I'd have believed Will," she said quietly. "I'd have believed anything he told me. I'd have believed in him if he hadn't told me anything, if he'd just expected me to trust him without words. But when he got absolutely furious and . . . and violent and insulting, when he marched out of the house like that, then I realized that what you'd said was . . . was probably true." She glanced at Chuck. "I hope you're pleased!"

He said uncomfortably: "I'm sorry, ma'am, I—"

"You've already said that. I don't believe it! I think the only person you're sorry for is yourself. The whole world is against you, isn't it, Mr. McAuliffe? Everybody's taking unfair advantage of you. . . . Well, let me ask you just one question: who started it? I can understand how you feel about losing your cattle, but why didn't you think of that before you sent them charging at a duly constituted posse enforcing the law of the land—"

"The law of the land!" he said, stung into anger again. "This quarantine, ma'am? Why, I'll bet half the folks who put that law through your state legislature didn't give a d—excuse me, didn't care a hoot about Spanish fever or protecting the poor farmers. They just saw a lot of Texas cattle coming up the trail and figured out a way to block them from market so they could get their hands on them cheap!"

She stared at him, aghast. "Why, you're quite mad! Oh, maybe here and there a few people have taken advantage of the quarantine for their own profit, but—" Abruptly she reached for the whip at her side. "No, sit still, I'm not going to hit you, Mr. McAuliffe!" she snapped, flicking the aged horse lightly across the flank. "I'm just going to show you something. You claim to be a cattleman, maybe you'll understand. Not that I really expect you to understand anything that doesn't affect *your* feelings or *your* pocketbook!"

25.

IT WAS A LARGE, well-kept farm some miles from town, but much of the stock in the fenced pasture, lean and poor-looking, didn't match up with the prosperous appearance of the place. Jean Kincaid drove right up to the house. A plump little man with a red, round face and silky white hair came out to greet them. His welcoming smile became less warm as he recognized the girl's companion.

"Good morning, Uncle Wayne," Jean said. Her expression was polite and innocent as she turned to Chuck. "Mr. McAuliffe, I believe you've met my uncle, Judge Thomson."

Chuck said grimly, "Yes'm, I made the judge's acquaintance in court yesterday morning."

The judge regarded Chuck without favor, and spoke to his niece: "Jeannie, girl, does your dad know you're gallivanting around the countryside with—"

The girl laughed. "Oh, I'm perfectly safe with Mr. McAuliffe. He hasn't got his big revolver back yet. . . . Uncle Wayne, do you mind if I show him around the place? Mr. McAuliffe thinks our concern over Texas fever is greatly exaggerated. He thinks our quarantine is just a sly Yankee plot to rob honest Texas citizens of their cattle. Oh, he admits we may have lost a few head here and there—"

"A few head!" The judge's voice was harsh. "Half my purebred herd is dead, thanks to that one bunch of scrawny longhorns that came through here! And those that have recovered . . . well, look at them!" He waved his hand toward the pasture. "And it's not over yet; new ones are still coming down with the fever. I've got the ailing stock penned up back of the barn. . . . Show the young man around, by all means! Just be careful of your pretty dress, it's kind of dusty and dirty back there. A Yankee trick, indeed!"

He marched back into the house, shaking his head. Jean Kincaid glanced at Chuck, but didn't speak. She guided the buggy around the building and through the ruts and dust of the farmyard. They didn't get out; it wasn't necessary. They sat there a while in silence; then the girl lifted the reins and spoke to the old horse and they drove away.

"Well, Mr. McAuliffe?" she murmured at last.

He retained in his mind a dismal picture of handsome cattle of some eastern breed standing glassy-eyed and staring, of cattle with arched backs and sagging heads staggering from weakness, of cattle tossing their heads in a kind of delirious frenzy. . . .

He cleared his throat and said, "I can't figure it. It must be something to which our south Texas stock is immune."

"We don't know what it is. But you've seen the result."

"Perhaps," he said reluctantly, "I spoke a mite hastily."

The girl said coolly, "It would seem to be a habit of yours."

No more was said, the whole way back to town. They met the sheriff, on his Indian pony, as they came to the square. He rode up to them and eyed them rather sharply, as if surprised to see them together, but asked no questions.

"I was setting out to look for you, McAuliffe; only I was delayed taking care of some trouble at the hotel—"

"Trouble?" Jean said. "What kind of trouble, Dad?"

"Nothing to concern you, Miss," her father said. He turned back to Chuck, who hoped his face did not betray uneasy knowledge. "Son, I did the best I could for you," the sheriff said. "Your fine and costs have been paid, and here's the balance of your money." He drew a cloth bag from his coat pocket, and grinned. "That Bristow—poor fellow, I feel kind of guilty now for the way I bluffed him—didn't much like my setting a bottom price. Maybe he was figuring on paying the court judgment and no more. But it occurred to me, if his partner could afford to offer your dad three dollars a head, like you told me, Mr. Bristow might pay the county the same, so I told him I wouldn't entertain any lower bids. Turned out, either he wasn't much of a poker player, or he wanted those cattle mighty bad." He held out the bag. "Here. It's not as much as you came from Texas to get, I know, but at least it's enough to pay your crew and get you home with something to spare."

Chuck took the money. He was aware that his ears were red. He didn't look at the girl on the seat beside him. He didn't have to look: she'd have the unbearable, triumphant, self-righteous expression of any female who'd been proved right twice in one morning. Then she stirred slightly, and he did look, and found himself mistaken again. She seemed pleased and mildly proud at this evidence of her father's cleverness, but she had matters of more compelling interest on her mind.

"Dad," she said, "what *is* the mystery? What happened at the hotel? Why are you sorry for Mr. Bristow?"

The sheriff hesitated, and shrugged his shoulders. "Well, you'll hear it anyway. Mrs. Bristow was found dead in her room just a short while ago."

Jean gasped, and put her hand to her mouth. "Dead? How terrible!" After a moment, she asked, "How did it happen?"

"A laudanum bottle was found beside her, empty," the sheriff said. "There's little doubt the poor young lady took her own life. Apparently there was a quarrel last night, and Bristow struck his wife and marched out—we have this from his partner, Paine, who was lying next door drunk—but woke up long enough to hear the end of the altercation. It seems that Mrs. Bristow wasn't happy about the footloose life they were leading, anyway. She'd been used to better things before her marriage. She'd been after her husband to settle down. Apparently, she became despondent after he left. . . ." He paused, and went on: "I have little sympathy for wife-beaters, but I can't help feeling for the man, having to live with the memory of that last blow. I've sent Paine to notify him. I'd have gone myself, only I have to ride over to Colliersville to pick up a prisoner." He held out his hand. "I'll say good-bye, McAuliffe."

Chuck took the sinewy hand. "Good-bye, sir."

"I've told Joe Breen, over at the jail, to give you back your outfit's guns when you come by." The sheriff turned to his daughter. "I won't be home before tomorrow night, probably."

"Do you have to go clear over to Colliersville, Dad? If it's just a matter of fetching a prisoner, can't you send—" Jean Kincaid seemed to hesitate over the name, "—can't you send Will?"

The sheriff shook his head. "Will's escorting Mr. Bristow and his twelve hundred longhorns across the line, with orders not to leave before he sees them pointed west towards the army posts. . . ."

The information, so casually delivered, sent a shock through Chuck, reminding him of the plans he'd made at his father's grave. Things were working out just right, it seemed. The sheriff was leaving town so he wouldn't be around to interfere. Will Reese was heading down into Indian Territory where his badge meant nothing. When the job was finished, he'd be riding back alone.

It'll be like shooting a duck on a millpond, Chuck remembered saying to Joe Paris. And with Reese taken care of, they could go after the cattle and Jack Keller— there was another score to be settled. It would be a tough proposition, a handful of Texas cowboys against all of Keller's bushwhackers, but with careful planning, and surprise in their favor, they stood a chance of pulling it off.

He should have felt a sense of pleasure and anticipation, but instead the whole proposed, violent business seemed strangely unlikely and unreal, like one of those wild notions you got in the middle of the night and laughed at in the morning. Chuck was aware that Sheriff Kincaid had ridden closer and leaned down to give his daughter a peck on the cheek. She threw her arms around his neck and gave him a hug and a kiss in return. The sheriff straightened up and cleared his throat, obviously embarrassed at having displayed so much sentimentality. He swung his pony around, threw up his hand in a farewell gesture, and rode off briskly.

It came to Chuck that these were good and kindly people who'd gone out of their way to be friendly when they'd had every reason to dislike and mistrust him. They'd taken him into their house when he was hurt, they'd tolerated his childish sulks, they'd been civil and helpful when he'd done nothing to deserve it. And in return he'd given them only hate and suspicion and wild, unfounded accusations. Even now, he was only waiting to get his hands on some weapons before embarking on a career of murder and robbery—and the fact that the men he was planning to rob and kill had committed crimes themselves didn't entitle him to step outside the law to deal with them.

"Sheriff!" he heard himself call. "Just a minute!"

Kincaid checked his pony and looked back. Chuck glanced at Jean, who interpreted his glance correctly, and sent the buggy ahead.

"What is it, son?" the sheriff asked as they came abreast.

Chuck drew a long breath. "There's something you ought to know, sir," he said. "There's something I'd better tell you. We were going to handle it ourselves —the crew and I—but I reckon it's more in your line of work. . . ."

26.

To MIGUEL APODACA, it was a simple matter. If one was sent to watch and listen, one watched and listened. The fact that the camp one was to spy upon was located in an open place and hard to approach unseen did not change the instructions issued by Joe Paris, who, in the absence of the young *patron,* was in charge.

"Keep an eye on that outfit," Joe had said. "Find out

what they're up to. I don't figure those cattle are bound
for any army posts. In particular, keep an eye on that
bearded fellow who called himself Netherton when we
found him along the trail—the one whose leg the Major
dug a bullet out of. He was at the auction, bold as brass,
going by the name of Bristow. And keep an eye on Mister
Reese, too. We don't want to lose him."

The *segundo* seemed to overestimate the number of
eyes available to one man, Miguel reflected wryly, as
he wormed his way along a shallow gully towards the
camp, after leaving his horse in a clump of trees at a
safe distance. Well, two eyes would have to serve; he was
fortunate to have that many, he thought grimly, touching the great scar on his face. He could still recall quite
clearly the terror that had come to him that morning
a year ago, after he had fought his way out of the
river into which he had been thrown for dead, when he
had found himself alone in desolate country, unarmed,
sick, and half-blind. . . .

It had been a dark, wet night when the Laughlin
outfit had been ambushed, and he had seen no faces and
heard no voices. There had been only the sudden crash of
gunfire all about them as they returned to camp unsuspecting after checking the stampede; that, and the tear-
ing impact of the bullet that had smashed him from the
saddle, then unconsciousness until he found himself in
water, strangling, drowning. . . . Well, the old *patron*
had taught the murderers one lesson, a few weeks back.
It could hardly be a different gang; the tactics had been
the same. Now they were here, it seemed, judging by the
presence of this man Netherton or Bristow. Perhaps, if
all went well, their education could be continued, maybe
this very night. In the meantime, one could watch with
the two available eyes, and listen with the two available
ears.

Miguel had never seen Netherton, since the man had
remained in his wagon throughout the time it had accompanied the McAuliffe herd—only the *señorita* had
shown herself—but it was not hard to locate, among the
figures by the fire, a tall, bearded man who favored one
leg. Reese was also easy to spot by the swaggering size
of him—the murderer of the old *patron,* with his fine
new pistol at his hip. The two were standing together,
talking.

In broad daylight, it was impossible to get close enough to hear what they said, at first. Then, apparently seeking privacy, they moved away from the fire a distance. The bearded man looked around for a place to sit, to ease his leg, and limped still farther from camp, to a suitable rock where he subsided with an expression of relief. Reese remained standing above him.

Miguel, crouching in the grass, took stock of the situation. There seemed to be no hidden sentries, and only a handful of men in the camp, plus a couple riding herd on the cattle. These latter two were too far away to be an immediate threat, although, being mounted, they would constitute a serious danger if, discovered, he should have to make a run for his horse.

He started worming his way forward, but before he had covered more than half the distance, his cautious approach was interrupted by the arrival of a rider in camp. He recognized the thin, black-clad man who had tried to buy the herd at an outrageous price. This one paused by the fire to pour himself a cup of coffee and drink it down; then, a little unsteady on his feet—as if from drinking or hard riding or both—he made his way to where Reese and the bearded man awaited him.

Miguel heard his first words: "I almost rode right past you, friends. I thought you'd be farther along. If I hadn't seen the smoke of the fire. . . ." His voice dropped, and his words became indistinguishable at the distance.

Carefully, as befitted one who had fought Comanches and Apaches and learned their silent ways, Miguel made his way through the tall grass until he was lying within twenty yards of the rock on which the bearded man was sitting. Twice, the deputy sheriff, facing him, had looked directly at him, but no Kansas farmer could see anything that was not moving violently and bright red to boot.

The bearded man was speaking. ". . . took laudanum, eh?" he said, and chuckled. "Like any dance-hall trollop feeling sorry for herself after a couple of whiskies? Well, these high-toned wenches live on their fancy notions, and those notions don't last long after they discover that a fist will bruise them just like anybody else. I must say, however, I didn't figure she'd go that way quite so soon. In a way, it's a pity. I was looking forward to . . ."

He did not finish the sentence. Presently the black-clad

man said in a noncommittal voice, "I left enough money
to have her taken care of properly, but it will look
strange if you don't make an appearance at the funeral.
She was supposed to be your wife."

"I'm not concerned with what looks strange to the
good people of Jepson, Preacher," the bearded man said.
"I don't expect to come that way again."

The one called Preacher shrugged. "Your choice." He
looked around. "Like I said, I expected to find you
farther along. What delayed you?"

"That's what I want to know!" the big deputy burst out,
like a man who'd been holding himself in check with
difficulty. "Hell, we could have made half a dozen miles
more before sundown if we'd kept on. Why are we
sitting still, Mr. Keller? If the sheriff should find us here,
not even across the line, he'd start wondering and asking
questions."

The bearded man said, "I thought you'd taken care of
the sheriff."

"Well, sure, Mr. Keller, the old fool's supposed to
be on his way to Colliersville on a legitimate errand—
I got the message a couple of days ago and arranged for it
to be delayed until we needed him out of the way. But
he's got a habit of popping up, which is why I'd like for
us to get well into Indian Territory. . . ."

"We're not going into Indian Territory," said the
man who was now being called Keller. Netherton, Bristow, and now Keller, Miguel reflected; one would think
the bearded one would have trouble keeping track of his
own identity.

The deputy looked shocked. "Not going. . . . What
do you mean, Mr. Keller?"

"The cattle should be rested and ready to move an
hour or two after dark," Keller said. "They won't take
kindly to being driven at night, but we'll have the rest
of the men here before then, to lend a hand. You'll
show us a trail to the north and east, Mr. Reese. . . ."

"North and east!" Reese cried. "Why, that will take
us right through the middle of . . . That wasn't in the
bargain! We were to head west along the Territory until
I could show you—"

Keller said, ignoring this: "We'll keep moving by
night so nobody'll see the dust. You know this country;
you'll guide us. It would be awkward if we should sud-

denly find ourselves driving better than a thousand Texas cattle through some farmer's vegetable patch. But I'm sure this country's not so thickly settled you can't get us through unseen. Pick a secluded place that we can reach before daylight, and we'll lay over there tomorrow. Another night drive should see us out of this neighborhood and well on our way towards the railroad. And if we should be stopped by a posse or a mob of angry settlers, Mr. Reese, you'll use your badge and your authority in our behalf."

"But—"

Keller's voice went on smoothly and relentlessly: "You'll reassure the good citizens that these are healthy animals that have been properly inspected and legally admitted into the state. You'll inform them that you'll arrest any person who interferes with our legal progress. By the time they learn the truth, we'll be miles away."

Reese's voice held a note of panic. "But I can't do that! I'll be recognized! They'll check with Sheriff Kincaid. I'll be ruined; I'll never be able to show my face—"

Keller said, "One can't make money without some small risk, Mr. Reese, and I'm paying you well. Pick a route by which we won't be stopped, and the problem won't arise."

"That wasn't the agreement we made!" Reese said hotly. "I told you I knew a place to the west where I could get you around the quarantine without anybody being the wiser—"

"To be sure," Keller said. "I know one, too. All I have to do is drive these mangy cattle clear to Colorado. Well, I don't intend to do that, Mr. Reese. This herd has been a jinx ever since I laid eyes on it. It's cost me more money than it should have, not to mention a game leg and a number of dead men. Now that I've got it, I want to cash in on it fast, and I'm going to do it without driving clear around the state of Kansas. I'm taking these cattle directly to the railroad, and you're showing me how!"

The big deputy's face was hard and ugly. His hand was close to the butt of his pistol. He said, "You never intended to drive west at all! You lied—"

Keller nodded sadly. "It's an unfortunate habit I have, Mr. Reese. I do prevaricate a little upon occasion. ...*Preacher!*"

The last word snapped like a command. Hiding in the grass, Miguel saw the deputy, in the act of drawing his pistol, glance quickly around—the behavior of a fool, Miguel reflected. One draws a weapon or one does not draw it, but one does not stop in the middle of the act to look around like a nervous maiden. There would have been time for a good man to make his play, but now the black-clad one, standing a little to the side, moved slightly, and a small pistol appeared in his hand.

"Stand quite still, Mr. Reese," Keller said. "The Preacher's got a little slow and rusty since his gambling days, but he's killed more than one man with those sleeve guns of his, and you make a big target." Keller rose deliberately from the rock, reached out, and removed the deputy's weapon from the holster. "So. Now I think we'd better unload this for you. The men seem to have noticed nothing amiss. I don't want to shame you before them by taking this handsome piece away from you, but you'll find it lighter to carry without all that lead in the cylinder—"

It happened without warning. Some signal must have been passed, but Miguel had not seen it. Now the bearded man simply turned and fired, and dirt exploded into Miguel's face.

"Come out of there with your hands up," Keller snapped, "or the next bullet won't miss. . . . Ah. I had a hunch our Texas friends wouldn't be giving up so easily."

As he got to his feet resignedly, Miguel saw a bunch of riders coming across the open space behind him, well spread out. One was leading his, Miguel's, horse. Finding it must have led them to suspect his presence, but it was still a disgraceful way to be caught, like a coyote in a trap, and he deserved what would doubtless happen to him now. The bearded one did not look like a merciful man.

27.

HAVING FINISHED what he had to say, Chuck Mc-
Auliffe sat back on the buggy seat without looking at
the girl beside him. It was none of her business, anyway;
this was between the sheriff and him.

Kincaid's face was stern. "You say this man and his
gang attacked your outfit and murdered your brother?"

"Yes, sir."

"Kind of late in mentioning it, aren't you, son?"

Chuck said, "I figured maybe you had a cousin at
Gettysburg." The sheriff frowned quickly. Chuck went
on, "Dad and I spoke to a sheriff near Baxter Springs
about it, but it seems the fellow had a son killed at Shiloh
—or maybe you call it Pittsburgh Landing. You might
say he was prejudiced. Didn't seem to consider a dead
rebel of much account. Came near throwing both of
us in jail for making wild accusations against respectable
Yankee citizens."

"I see your point," Kincaid said wryly. "It would
hardly inspire confidence in the local law. So you were
going to handle it yourself, and take care of Will Reese
into the bargain? Not to mention taking back your cattle?"

"Yes, sir. Actually, Will Reese came first in our reckon-
ing. We didn't know at the time that Keller would be
taking the herd. We didn't even know his real name, then,
or what he was hanging around here for."

"You were just going to take it back from whoever
bought it, after settling with Will, is that it?"

"Yes, sir. We figured we had the right. Leastways,
we'd have the guns, and the two seem to go together, in
Indian Territory."

"I see." The sheriff looked grimly at Chuck. "Just
what made you up and change your mind, son?"

Chuck hesitated. It was a hard question to answer.
He could hardly say that he had somehow come to the
realization that there was more to growing up than just
learning what to do in bed with a woman, although that
was certainly part of it.

He said, "Well, there didn't seem to be any end to it,
sir."

"What do you mean?"

Chuck moved his shoulders in a kind of shrug. "Well, suppose I was to settle with Will Reese for killing the Old Man. Then I'd settle with this Keller for killing Dave. Then, to make a clean sweep, I ought to go back east and find the Yankee soldier who got my brother Jim at Gaines' Mill, oughtn't I? And maybe I ought to figure out who was responsible for Ma dying. . . ." He shrugged again. "You see what I mean? Do it right, and I'd have a lifetime job on my hands. It doesn't mean I don't want those fellows punished, but you're paid for such work, sheriff, and I've got other things to do. As for the cattle, with this money you got us, we'll come home in fair shape if not exactly rich, and there's plenty more steers in Texas. Twelve hundred longhorns aren't worth turning outlaw for, the way I see it."

The sheriff said, "You understand, there's nothing I could do about Will Reese, even if I wanted to. Think what you like about it, nobody's ever going to prove in court that he wasn't just an officer of the law doing his duty."

Chuck said, after a moment, "If he can live with it, I reckon I can."

"This other man, however . . . You're sure he called himself Keller? Jack Keller?"

"Yes, sir."

"The name is familiar to me, although he's never operated in these parts before, to my knowledge. He's one of those . . . well, there's been a lot of politics riding with these border gangs, but public opinion is turning against them, now that they can no longer hide their crimes under even a thin cloak of patriotism. I don't promise I can get Mr. Keller for a murder committed down in the Territory, but I think I can say with confidence that his marauding days are numbered."

"That's good enough for me," Chuck said.

"It may be," the sheriff said, "but will it be good enough for your men? They were mighty hot under the collar when they left town."

"I'll do my best," Chuck said mildly, "to persuade them to my way of thinking, Sheriff."

Kincaid looked at him hard for a moment, and nodded. "See that you do. Anything else on your mind?"

Chuck hesitated. He would have liked to unburden himself of certain memories concerning the girl who had killed herself, but not in the presence of Jean Kincaid. Anyway, there were some things a man didn't talk about. He'd have to work it out with his own conscience, somehow. There was, after all, no real crime involved; it was none of the sheriff's business.

"No, sir," he said. "That's about it."

"I'll be on my way, then," Kincaid said. He caught the question in Chuck's look, and grinned briefly. "Don't worry, son. I'm not neglecting Jack Keller, even if I seem to be riding off on other business. I've got a reason for wanting to be seen heading out of town peacefully. There's all kinds of ways of getting into a house besides walking through the front door."

He wheeled his pony and departed at a trot. Beside Chuck, Jean Kincaid picked up the reins.

"Where can I let you off, Mr. McAuliffe?"

"Right up there at the livery stable, if you don't mind, ma'am," Chuck said.

They rode the short distance in silence. She brought the buggy to a halt in front of the place. He started to climb out.

"Mr. McAuliffe."

"Yes'm?"

"I . . . I'm glad you had the good sense to give up your crazy scheme."

He stepped to the ground, and looked up at her, sitting there. "Crazy, ma'am?" he said. "I don't know about that. There'll be those who'll say we're crazy for riding home humbly without avenging our dead or collecting more than a fraction of the money we came all this way to get. I'll probably hear something like that from my own crew." He shrugged his shoulders. "They could even be right."

Her eyes widened slightly, the way they did when she was getting angry. He was coming to know the expression well.

"How can murder and robbery be right?"

He grinned at her lazily, knowing the grin would annoy her further. "In these parts, it seems to depend on who gets murdered and robbed, ma'am. I wasn't thinking much about right, anyway. It was just that, after a good look at Mister Keller, I didn't figure I wanted to get into the same line of business. It would have been the same if he'd been a banker or barber."

She glared at him, speechless, and shook the reins to

send the buggy away, without saying good-bye. He stepped back, removing his hat politely, and watched her drive off, regretting a little that he'd succumbed to the temptation to make her mad. But apparently it wasn't enough for a woman that you did a thing. To satisfy her, you had to wrap it up in a sanctimonious speech about right and wrong.

Well, it wasn't as if Jean Kincaid's opinion was a matter of great importance. After all, it was only last night that he'd asked another girl to marry him. To be sure, that girl was now dead, but respect for her memory alone should keep him from looking at other females for a decent interval—not that he'd be concerned about what a sharp-tongued Yankee miss thought of him, in any case.

28.

THE PONY was still a trifle lame from being knocked off its feet by Will Reese's big gray, so Chuck took it easy, riding south from town. He reached the crew's camp in the middle of the afternoon. It was located by a small spring in a pleasant grove of trees, with an open meadow for the horses close at hand.

He dismounted by the spring, splashed water on his face, drank sparingly, and straightened up to untie the heavy bundle lashed to his saddle. He passed this to Joe Paris, who had come up to greet him.

"There are your weapons," he said. "I've arranged for provisions at the store; Coosie can pick them up with the wagon. He'd better hitch up right now or he won't be back before midnight. Everything's paid for; all he has to do is load up and come right back."

He swung back to attend to his mount, limping slightly. Joe Paris asked, behind him: "What happened to you, kid? You didn't have that cut lip when we saw you last, and you move like a couple more horses had run over you."

"Why," Chuck said without turning his head, "I got licked, I reckon. Anyway, when it was over, I was down and the other fellow was up."

"That big deputy again?"

Chuck nodded, hooking the stirrup over the saddle
horn so he could get at the cinches. He was aware that
the rest of the crew had gathered around. They'd be
eager for action after a day's inactivity. They'd expect
unhesitating leadership from him, after his violent words
at his father's grave. It occurred to him that, lately, he
seemed to be forever tripping over the consequences of
having talked too much and too loudly. Maybe it would
be a good idea if he practiced keeping his mouth shut
now and then.

"What happened?" Paris asked.

"Sheriff Kincaid stopped the fight, if you want to call
it a fight," Chuck said shortly. He glanced around.
"Where's Mike?"

"He's trailing the herd," Joe said. "We've been kind
of keeping an eye on things, waiting for you. One of the
boys even slipped over to watch the auction. That Netherton fellow was there, calling himself Bristow."

"His real name is Jack Keller," Chuck said.

"Well, whatever his name is, that Yankee sheriff got
him to pay three dollars a head for those steers. Did the
sheriff pass any of it along to you, or did he keep it all
for himself?"

Chuck patted his saddlebag. "I've got it all here,
except for the fine and what I paid out for supplies. The
sheriff's all right."

Joe Paris laughed. "I declare, we're likely to come out
of this in pretty good shape, after all. We'll take those
cattle back, like you said, sneak them up to the railroad
somehow—they can't be watching the whole Kansas
border—and get a good price for them there to add to
Mr. Keller's money. We'll be fixed to buy all of Texas,
time we get home." He chuckled. "Damn, if that won't
be a joke on the Yankees, selling them the same cattle
twice."

Chuck asked, "How many men has Keller got riding
with him?"

"Just an average crew, six or eight hands and that
deputy sheriff, last I heard."

"He had more than that down at the Arkansas. The
rest must be hiding out somewhere so as not to arouse
suspicion."

"Well, we licked them once, we can lick 'em again,"
Joe said. "I must say, I'm mighty pleased at the way it's

worked out. I wasn't looking forward to jumping a bunch
of honest cattlemen, Yankees or no; but I don't figure
to spend many sleepless nights over what happens to
this Keller and his friends. They're long overdue, the way
I see it."

Chuck stripped the saddle and blanket from his pony,
frowning. He was stalling and he knew it; and the longer
he waited, the harder it would get.

Joe Paris said cheerfully, "I've got to hand it to you,
youngster. The deputy went right along with them, just
like you figured he would. Better throw that saddle on
a horse that isn't lame. Mike's going to let us know as
soon as Reese starts back to town. You'll get a chance
to pay him back for those bruises, with a gun in your
hand." The foreman hesitated, and went on: "I've been
thinking over what you said at the Major's grave, and
you're right about the way to do it. A backshooting
murderer like that doesn't deserve an even break. We'll
just finish him off like any coyote, and go after the herd."

There was a little pause. Chuck, still holding his saddle, swung about to face them. "We're not finishing anybody off," he said.

Joe Paris frowned quickly. "But—"

"And we're not stealing any cattle," Chuck said deliberately. "We're spending the night right here while the
cook fetches our grub and ammunition from town—
Coosie, you'd better start hitching up—and in the morning we're saddling up and heading for home."

He kept his gaze on Joe, because the foreman was
the one to convince, but he was aware that his words
weren't being received with favor by the other men.
There was a little stir of disapproval throughout the
group.

Paris said quickly, "It was your own idea, kid—"

"That's right," Chuck admitted. "I'd just buried my
pa and I wasn't feeling too happy about it; and I guess
I shot off my mouth some about the big mean things
I was going to do. But I've had a day to simmer down,
and I'm taking back what I said. We're not going to turn
murderers and outlaws just because we've run into a
little bad luck. The sheriff's an honest man, and he has
all the information I could give him. He'll settle with
Mister Keller; apparently the law's been after that *hombre*
for a long time. As for Reese, I don't love him any more

than I ever did, but he was within his legal rights when he used his gun, and drygulching him isn't going to bring the Old Man back. The Old Man wouldn't even like it if he knew about it."

Joe said quickly, "All right, then we'll take him in the open! But I'm not leaving here with the Major's killer alive!"

Chuck said, "We're heading back to Texas, old-timer. Coosie, damn you, I told you to start getting that wagon ready!"

There was a brief silence. He could feel them all against him. The cook, burly and bald, had recovered his bullying assurance in the weeks that had passed since he'd had to seek shelter in the muddy Arkansas. He stepped forward heavily and said, "Don't you swear at me, young fellow! I wouldn't have taken it from your daddy, and I sure ain't taking it from you! If you ask me, you're getting a mite too big for your britches, telling grown men what to—"

Chuck swung the saddle, with a mighty two-handed effort. It caught the larger man alongside the head. The cook staggered. The spring was behind him. Too late, he felt the drop-off and tried to catch himself, arms flailing; then he sat down in twelve inches of water with a resounding splash. His discomfiture brought a ripple of involuntary laughter from men who'd had to put up with his greasy cooking and surly ways. Chuck wheeled to face them.

"This is a McAuliffe outfit," he said, breathing hard, "and my name's McAuliffe. Now, you can ride south with me in the morning, or I'll pay you off right here, but one thing's for sure: any murdering you do, you do on your own time! All right, Joe, which is it to be?"

Joe Paris glanced at the cook, who was hauling himself out of the spring, snorting and dripping. Paris chuckled and the remaining tension went out of the group.

"You've got mighty convincing ways, Mr. McAuliffe," he said. "Just take it easy with that saddle; I'm an old man and I've had my bath for this year. Another would likely kill me."

They were all grinning now. Chuck filled his lungs with air. "We ride for Texas?"

Paris laughed. "The Major always said you'd be hard to handle if you ever started feeling your oats. Watch that Chuck boy of mine, he'd say; the kid ain't much for big but he's hell for smart. All right, *amigo*. He was your dad. I reckon you've got the right to say—"

There was a crackle of sound at the edge of the grove. Joe stopped speaking. All the men instinctively moved nearer the weapons that had been deposited on the ground at the foreman's feet.

"Rider coming in," somebody said.

They caught a glimpse of movement, and Joe said, "Hell, it's Mike's buckskin. . . . that's funny! Why's Mike spooking around like that! Why doesn't he ride right in?"

Then the buckskin horse came slowly into full sight, and they saw that it carried no rider. The bridle-reins were twisted about the saddle horn. Even before the animal reached them, they could see the blood on the saddle.

29.

WAITING ON the ridge, in the fading light, Chuck felt the bitterness of a man whose good resolutions had been nullified by a malicious fate. If Joe Paris had just minded his business and hadn't sent Miguel . . . Chuck grimaced. If he, Chuck, had just kept quiet instead of blowing off like a windy fool, Joe might never have thought of shadowing the herd with the idea of later reclaiming it by force, and Mike wouldn't be in trouble or dead. Fate made a handy excuse, but there generally wasn't much substance to it, when you looked at it hard.

Below him, he could see Keller's camp, a couple of miles distant, out in the open in a long, shallow, grassy valley. Off to the right, where the valley narrowed, was the herd with a couple of riders on guard. It was a calm and peaceful scene, and instinct warned him that it was false as a harlot's smile—he'd heard the simile used once as a boy, and he remembered asking his mother what a harlot was. She'd been quite taken aback, he recalled; and then she'd said that a harlot was a very bad woman. There were two kinds of women, she'd said, good and bad, and she hoped he'd grow up having nothing to do with the bad.

His brother Dave, on the other hand, had thought he needed education; and now he had a pretty good idea what kind of education Dave had had in mind. There seemed to be two viewpoints in this matter, the male and the female; and trying to reconcile them didn't look promising. It seemed to be a matter, like so many others, in which a man—as long as his loyalty was not committed elsewhere—could do what seemed necessary, or even just what seemed desirable, as long as he refrained from talking about it afterwards.

"Pssst!" It was Joe Paris, below and behind him. "Sam's back. Come on down."

He eased himself back from the skyline cautiously, before he stood up and hurried down to where the foreman was standing. Sam Biederman was there, too. The big, blond rider had a worn and sweaty look. The rest of the crew was lounging nearby.

"See anything from up there?" Joe asked.

Chuck shook his head. "Never saw a cow camp look so innocent."

"They've got Mike. He's alive," Joe said. "Tell him, Sam."

"I worked in close," Biederman said. "They have no guards near the camp, no sentries. But Miguel they have, hanging by the wrists from the wagon tongue, propped high. That man with the fine beard, he should an Apache be. Little cuts with a knife he makes, here, there, and he laughs, haha. Then Mike spits, ptuie, and the bearded one strikes with the fist so that Mike hangs there without life. They were trying to revive him with water when I came away."

There was a murmur from the men. Chuck asked, "Could you hear what Keller wanted?"

"I was not close enough. Questions he asked, but he got no answer from Miguel."

Joe Paris said, "I had him tagged for a mean one at first, with that scar on his face. But now I find I've got to get him out of there."

"To be sure," Chuck said, "but it will take doing."

"I have an idea," the foreman said. "If we circle around to the west end of the valley, we'll have the herd between us and the camp. We can get those steers to running, and send them right through the camp, and follow them in. The wagon will give Miguel some protection.

We'll have him cut loose and out of there before the dust settles."

Chuck said dryly, "Mister Keller would never think of us trying a plan like that, naturally."

Joe looked at him sharply. "What are you driving at, boy?"

"Doesn't look like much of a crew down there," Chuck said. "Where are the rest of Keller's men?"

Joe said, "We beat them up some at the Arkansas, and wounded Keller himself. Scum like that doesn't stick with a man who leads them into a deadfall. It could be this is all he has left."

"Maybe," Chuck said, "but he seemed mighty cocky and confident when I talked with him in Jepson, confident enough to warn me off like he expected to make it stick —and he knows how many there are of us. And then there's the question of who tied up the reins of Mike's horse so he'd drift back to camp, and who smeared blood artistically over Mike's saddle so we'd come charging to the rescue. And there's Mike himself, hung up right in plain sight where any of us scouting around will be bound to see him being abused. And there's the known fact that Mister Keller is a man who's got a real fondness for ambushes. I figure this is a trap and Mike's the bait. The big question is, what does Keller expect us to do?"

"Even so—"

Chuck said, "Mister Keller is also a man who's aware that Texas cattle have been known to stampede upon occasion. He's even taken advantage of the fact himself, once or twice. It's the big weakness of any cow outfit. He'd hardly expect us to overlook it—with him camped right out there in the open, an inviting target for a bunch of wild steers. I figure the narrow end of that valley, down where that herd is, has more men and rifles right now than it has rabbits. He's waiting for us to strike there."

Joe Paris said dubiously, "You're doing an awful lot of figuring, seems to me."

Chuck said, "We're up against a figuring man. It's up to us to out-figure him."

"And how are you planning to do that?"

Chuck asked, "Sam, just how many men did you count down at the camp itself?"

"Why, there was Keller, the deputy, that fellow in black, and four others."

"Seven in all," Chuck said. "I guess he figures that's enough to discourage any direct attack. But that one they call the Preacher drinks pretty hard. I don't figure he'll be much account; and I don't expect our deputy friend, Reese, will be too eager to fight anybody else's battles. There are five of us. . . ."

He frowned thoughtfully, working it out in his head. It wasn't a kind of calculation he'd ever had to make before, and he was surprised that these older men, with their experience of war and battle, should be waiting respectfully to hear what he had to say. Then he understood. They were McAuliffe riders, as he'd pointed out to them earlier, and they were waiting for a McAuliffe to give the orders. They might not have the confidence in him that they'd had in the Old Man—with good reason —but he'd made his claim to leadership and they were prepared to let him prove it, if he could.

30.

DARKNESS WAS slow in coming. Waiting wasn't easy. Chuck found himself remembering that once he'd envied these men who'd known the excitement and glory of war. In actuality, he understood now, it must have been very much like this: a lot of waiting, a lot of wondering what it would be like to stop a bullet, a lot of worrying about whether you were up to the task you'd been set—whether you'd figured things out right or made a mistake that would get a lot of men killed. It was no wonder the Old Man had come back changed, unable, with other things on his mind, to make allowances for the tender feelings of one fool boy.

Lying there, watching the sky turn dark above him, Chuck found himself wishing for the Old Man back, if only just for a minute or two, just long enough so he could tell him . . . But it was too late for that. The time to speak, he knew now, was when you first had the impulse and the chance. You couldn't be sure the opportunity would ever come again.

It was dark enough now—or would be by the time they got into position—and he sat up and put his hat straight on his head. He pulled out the Remington pistol and checked the percussion caps and shoved the weapon back into the holster.

"Well," he said, "I reckon Lacey and Turkey might as well be on their way." He looked at the two men. "All you want to do is make noise," he said. "Don't expose yourselves needlessly, and don't worry about the herd. If it runs, fine, but if those brutes are feeling stubborn, don't get yourselves killed trying to get them moving. Just make the fellows up there *think* you're trying to start a stampede. If I'm right, they're expecting it, and it won't take much to start them shooting. As soon as your ruckus starts, down the valley, we'll hit the camp and try to get Miguel out."

Turkey LeBow, still favoring the arm through which he'd been shot at the Arkansas, climbed into the saddle and looked down at Chuck skeptically.

"I don't know about this," he said. "Sending us every which way. . . . There's seven men in that camp, and only three of you, remember."

Lacey Wills, a small, round, cheerful, bowlegged rider, said, "Ah, hell, it's as good a plan as any. If we start counting noses we'll be too scared to move. Come on, Turkey."

Chuck watched the two men ride off. He turned to the remaining two. "You've got it straight? The way I see it, they'll be expecting us to try to follow the cattle in, taking advantage of the dust and confusion like Joe said. Instead, we'll hit them before the herd ever moves, if it does move. We'll ride straight for Miguel. Joe and I will hold them off while Sam cuts him down and gets him away—you can handle him alone, even if he's unconscious, can't you, Sam?"

"Yes, I handle him," the big man said. "He is not so heavy; I carry him with one hand."

"Two will do, for a choice," Chuck said. "Just make it fast. We won't be wanting to hang around and socialize with those bushwhackers. . . . Joe, what's on your mind?"

"It's a crazy idea," the foreman said. Then he grinned abruptly. "But I'm damned if I can think of a better. . . ."

Then they were moving at last, which was a relief. Joe led the way, taking advantage of the contours of the land to bring them towards the camp unseen in the deepening twilight. Every so often Keller's campfire would be visible ahead of them with figures standing about it. It seemed incredible that one of those figures would not look up and see them and give the alarm, but none did. Presently Joe halted in the shelter of a patch of brush.

"I figure this is as close as we'd better go until the music starts," the foreman said softly. "Oh. Here's something you may find a use for."

He held out a revolver that gleamed dully in the darkness. Chuck took it, and looked at the foreman questioningly.

"It's Dave's, the mate to the one you're packing," Joe said. "Sometimes five shots ain't quite enough. Stick it in your belt. It's loaded and capped. I've got the Major's. Hope you have no objections."

"No," Chuck said. "Of course I have no objections."

"Keep that extra weapon in reserve," Joe said. "Nothing looks as foolish as a man trying to shoot two guns at once. You know what I miss at a time like this?"

"No," Chuck said. "What?"

"That damned old cavalry saber. Never could do much damage with one, I'll admit, but it gave a man something to hold onto after he'd shot his firearms empty. . . . What is it, Sam?"

"Miguel. I saw him move. At least there is still life in him."

"Well, don't stop to take his pulse when we get in there," Joe said dryly. "I wonder what's holding up the other boys. Maybe they've stopped for a hand of poker or something."

It occurred to Chuck that the foreman was talking just a little too much, perhaps just to reassure the youngest member of the party—but perhaps the older man, even though he'd experienced many situations like this in his lifetime, also felt a certain constriction of the chest, a certain dryness of the mouth. It was a comforting thought. Chuck glanced at Sam Biederman and saw that even that normally stolid and phlegmatic rider was fiddling with his equipment in an unnecessary manner. Apparently his own sensations weren't absolutely unique. . . .

The first shot came without warning. It sounded thin and far away. Then they heard the distant *yip-yip-yipee* of a cowboy trying to urge reluctant cattle into motion;

and suddenly that whole end of the valley seemed to explode with gunfire.

Joe Paris let out a long breath, listening. "I sure hope those boys are keeping their heads down. Must be a dozen guns going off down there."

"Yes," Chuck said. "Well, I reckon it's our turn now."

There wasn't any sense sitting around thinking about it; and for this last short ride Joe's experience as an Indian fighter and cavalry scout was hardly needed to guide them. There was, in fact, no excuse for Chuck Mc-Auliffe's not getting the hell out there in front where he belonged and leading them straight into this trouble he'd picked out for them to sample. . . . Rather to his surprise, he found himself doing just that, kicking his horse into a run. His pistol was in his hand, but he did not shoot, not even after he was well within range. A gunshot would attract attention, and, engrossed with the fireworks down the valley, they hadn't seen him yet.

Charging in, Chuck got a brief picture of the camp in the firelight. Miguel was hanging motionless from the wagon tongue, ignored. Will Reese and Paine—whom he'd last seen in Amanda Netherton's room—stood close together by the fire. Some of the other hands had moved a little out of the light where their vision would not be impaired. One man had just brought up a horse for Jack Keller, who was preparing to mount.

It was Keller who saw him first. As the bearded man's face turned towards him, Chuck swung his pistol up and fired. Keller's horse reared, breaking free of the man who held it; Keller himself managed to get a foot in the stirrup and a hand on the horn and was carried out of the light in this manner by the wildly bucking animal. Another man turned and fired at the oncoming riders. Chuck shot again and missed, and the gun-flame almost scorched his face as he rode the man down. The rest were all running now, scattering into the darkness. Behind him, he heard Joe Paris' revolver speak. Joe's voice shouted, with the bark of a cavalry sergeant:

"Back here, kid! Keep your mount under control, damn it!"

Chuck wheeled his pony. Somebody shot at him from outside the circle of firelight and he fired back. That was three loads gone out of five, he reminded himself. The big figure of Sam Biederman was at the wagon, knife in hand. A shadowy shape showed beyond, and Chuck spurred his pony hard and fired again. A gun blazed in answer, and he shot at the flash and shoved the empty pistol into the holster and snatched out the extra gun Joe had given him—Dave's gun. There was no difference in the balance of the weapons. His pony, charging past Sam Biederman, shied at something on the ground: a dark, inert, human shape. Apparently one of his bullets, at least, had found a target.

He cut back again, and passed Joe Paris—the two of them weaving a protective pattern in front of the wagon —and there was a new sound in the air: a rumbling, threatening sound, like that of an avalance starting down the mountain.

"There go those damn longhorns!" Chuck shouted. "Sam, get going! They're off and running! They're headed this way!"

Sam had the limp figure of Miguel across his horse, and was swinging into the saddle. Chuck heard a bullet go by with a nasty, cracking sound. He saw the flare of the muzzle-flame from the corner of his eye, and twisted to shoot back.

"Come on, kid! Time to leave!" Joe Paris shouted.

The rumble of the stampede was louder now. Sam Biederman was riding off into the dark, with Joe hovering protectively behind him. Chuck started to follow, but the wind of a bullet beat against his ear, and he looked back to see a rider come past the fire at a dead run—a bearded man on a tall bay horse. The flash of this man's gun was round and orange as he shot again.

Chuck hauled his pony around and took careful aim. *Don't think about it, or worry about whether it's right or wrong,* Amanda Netherton had said. At the moment, the advice seemed moderately superfluous. When the sights were steady and clear in the firelight, he pressed the trigger, and Dave's pistol fired. Jack Keller spilled from the saddle, and now the ground was shaking with the thunder of the stampede, and the lead steers were lunging into the light, and it was time to leave for sure.

He caught up with Joe and Sam Biederman near the foot of the north ridge. They stopped in the willows by a small stream. Chuck and Joe dismounted and went for-

ward to take Miguel as Sam eased him down. The little
Mexican rider stirred.

"Mother of God!" he said irritably. "That is no way
to ride a horse! What does that big Dutchman think, that
I am part of his saddle?"

Joe chuckled. "Well, I don't reckon we have to worry
about him. He's too tough to—"

He broke off abruptly, reaching for his gun, but a voice
from the bushes said sharply: "Hold it, Texan. You're
covered by six rifles!" The voice was familiar, and Chuck
recognized the lean shape of Sheriff Kincaid, coming
forward through the darkness. "I thought you were on
your way home, son," the sheriff said irritably. "I told
you I was taking care of it, didn't I? What do you mean,
busting in here in front of my posse and raising hell? I
ought to arrest the whole lot of you!"

31.

THE BUGGY came across the meadows in the middle of
the morning, giving a wide berth to the grazing cattle.
There was nothing in the peaceful scene to arouse
memories of the violence of two nights before, except
some hoofprints in the earth, and, down the valley, an
overturned and half-burned wagon—the stampeding herd
had shoved it over into the fire.

Sheriff Kincaid stopped the buggy in the shade of
the nearest trees, spoke to the girl beside him, got out,
and walked over to the McAuliffe wagon, which had
been brought up to this place. Chuck, who'd scrambled to
find a shirt when he realized the sheriff was not alone,
heard him speak to Turkey LeBow, who was mending
gear by the fire.

"Your Mexican friend is getting along fine," Kincaid
said. "He says not to worry, he'll catch up with you,
wherever you are, as soon as the doctor lets him out of
bed." There was a little pause, as if the sheriff were
looking around for someone. "Where's McAuliffe?"

"The Old Man?" Turkey said. "Why, he was here
just a minute ago. . . ."

Chuck stood quite still for a moment. In the parlance

of the trail, the boss of the outfit was the Old Man, re-
gardless of age. . . . Chuck drew a deep breath, tucked
his shirt in, and came around the wagon.

"Well, we got the cattle rounded up for you again,
sheriff," he said. "It was the least we could do, after
upsetting your plans."

The sheriff shrugged. "As it turned out, it made no
real difference. Keller's dead; we're rid of him. I did
want to see which way they'd move before I closed in on
them; but we have the testimony of your rider to the
effect that they were planning to violate the quarantine,
and some of the men we rounded up are beginning to
talk to save their skins. By the time they come to trial,
we'll have worse crimes to hang on them than driving a
bunch of steers the wrong direction." Kincaid hesitated.
"Will Reese got away. I got word this morning that a
man of his description had been seen joining up with a
party heading for the gold fields. I don't figure we'll see
him again." The sheriff glanced towards the buggy under
the trees. "There's nothing for him to come back to
here, that's for sure."

Chuck said, "I guess it's just as well, although some
of the men would still like to get their hands on him."

"Now, about these cattle," the sheriff said. "There's
no question about ownership. Whatever Keller was, they
were legally acquired by him, and this man Paine we
have in jail seems to've been his legal partner, with
papers to prove it. No doubt they fixed it that way for
some swindle or other, but that's the way it stands. So
Mr. Paine owns these longhorns. However, he isn't
likely to be taking an active part in the livestock business
any time soon, and it seems like he's willing to part with
the herd at a reasonable price. Three dollars a head was
the figure he mentioned—that would give him back the
money his partner paid out, to use for hiring a lawyer
and such. I reckon you could drive the price down a bit
if you had a mind. Mister Paine is hardly in a position
to bargain."

Chuck found himself remembering a dismal hotel
room, and the still figure in the bed, and the Preacher's
voice saying: *I was . . . quite fond of her, myself. In a
fatherly way, of course.* He owed the man in jail a debt
of sorts. Certainly, he did not want to take advantage of
the other's troubles.

He said, "I'd like to pay Mr. Paine's price in full, Sheriff. However, I simply haven't got that much left. There was the fine to pay and provisions to buy. . . ."

Kincaid said, "Well, it just so happens I have a few hundred dollars saved up for a likely investment. I figure between us we can manage to meet the figure, that is, if you don't mind going shares with a Yankee. . . . Oh, I'm not handing out charity, son. I got some more news. Seems there's a fellow named McCoy who's got an arrangement with the railroad for shipping cattle from a small town out north and west of here somewhere."

"West?" Chuck asked quickly. "Here in Kansas?"

The sheriff chuckled. "I thought you'd prick up your ears. That's right, I said west, outside the quarantine area, or at least out where there's hardly any settlement to bother you. You head west until you hit an old trail used by Jesse Chisholm, the trader, and follow it north to the railroad. . . . Abilene, that's the name of the town. Mr. Joseph G. McCoy, in Abilene, Kansas. He's sent out handbills asking for cattle. Says he can ship them as fast as they come. Good prices, too, twenty-five to thirty-five dollars a head. So you see, I expect to get my money back with a profit."

Chuck said, "You will, sir! And thank you—"

The sheriff said gruffly, "It's a business proposition pure and simple, no call for thanks. Well, I could use a cup of that coffee. . . . No, no, I'll help myself."

He turned to the fire. After a moment, Chuck left him there and moved across the grassy space to the buggy under the trees. Seeing him come, Jean Kincaid stepped down to meet him on the ground, but for some reason neither of them spoke a conventional greeting when he reached her. This morning, he saw, she was wearing a white shirtwaist and a blue wool skirt. Her hair was uncovered. Here in the shade, it seemed to shine with a soft light of its own. He was startled to realize that she was beautiful. It seemed odd that he hadn't noticed it before.

There was a little pause. He cleared his throat, and asked, "Would you care for a cup of coffee?"

She shook her head. "Are those the wild Texas cattle I've been hearing about? They look quite dangerous."

He said, "Well, I wouldn't venture among them on foot, ma'am." Looking at her, he was suddenly very

thankful that he was not fleeing through Indian Territory
with a stolen herd of cattle and a price on his head, or
even just standing there with Will Reese's blood on his
hands—whatever she might think of Reese now, she'd
been going to marry him once. If he'd been killed, she'd
always have remembered who killed him. Chuck said
abruptly, "Your dad's been kind enough to offer to help
me buy back my herd. After I've sold it, I'll have to come
back this way to repay—"

He found himself flushing. The words weren't coming
right; and after all, he'd only known her a couple of days.
Some people might even question whether he had the
right to speak.

She was smiling. "*Have* to, Mr. McAuliffe?" she
murmured. "Why, if it's inconvenient, I'm sure you
could arrange to send Dad his money."

He looked at her for a moment. She was teasing him,
and he wasn't in a mood to be teased. "I could," he said
shortly. "What I'm trying to find out from you, ma'am, is
whether or not it will be worth my while to come back.
If not, I reckon we'll take the straight trail home from
this Abilene place, so we'll know it for future drives."

He thought she'd get mad, being spoken to so bluntly;
instead, she shook her head abruptly and said, very
quietly, "I'm sorry. I didn't mean to . . . I would like for
you to come back. I'll be waiting."

He looked at her for a moment longer, memorizing the
way she looked for the miles ahead. He would have liked
to kiss her, and perhaps she was expecting it, but it
wouldn't have seemed quite right yet. There was still a
matter to be settled between him and his conscience;
there were things that had happened that had to be
studied out before he could live with them comfortably.
He lifted his hat, and turned quickly and walked to his
horse, and swung into the saddle.

"Joe!" he shouted. "Joe Paris! We're back in the
cattle business. Do you know a town called Abilene?"

Across the meadow, Joe called back, "Abilene?
Where's that?"

"We'll find out when we get there," Chuck called.
He rose in the stirrups and waved his arm. "Start 'em
moving west, I'll be along as soon as I've signed some
papers for the sheriff here."

He heard the cook, behind him, grumbling and fuming

about folks who expected a man to break camp without warning. Before him, the herd was starting into motion, the lead steers finding their accustomed places at the point, the pioneers of a movement that within ten years would stock a continent with Texas beef. But the longhorned animals didn't know they were pioneers, and neither did Chuck McAuliffe. He only knew that he had a girl waiting, and that, in this summer of 1867, he was taking a herd of cattle to a place called Abilene that he'd never heard of until five minutes ago. And if they didn't want his cattle there, he'd take them somewhere else. . . . But history says they did.